Selected Stories of
Munshi Premchand

Translation by

Sudha Narasimhachar

Publisher
UNICORN BOOKS

F-2/16, Ansari Road, Daryaganj, New Delhi-110002
☎ 011-23275434, 23262683, 23250704 • *Fax:* 011-23257790
E-mail: info@unicornbooks.in • *Website:* www.unicornbooks.in

Branch : Mumbai

23-25, Zaoba Wadi, Thakurdwar, Mumbai-400002
☎ 022-22010941, 022-22053387
E-mail: rapidex@bom5.vsnl.net.in

ISBN 978-81-7806-389-8

Printed at : Param Offsetters, Okhla, New Delhi-110020.

Contents

The importance of stories 1
1. *Bade Ghar Ki Beti* - The Rich Man's Daughter 4
2. The Salt Inspector 14
3. The Two Brothers 24
4. *Pancha Parameshwar* - Parameshwar the Arbitrator 31
5. *Boodhi Kaki* - The Old Aunt 43
6. Revenge 52
7. The Chess Players 63
8. *A Seer* and Quarter of Wheat 75
9. The Temple and the Mosque 83
10. *Manthra* - Panecea 95
11. Kazhaki 110
12. Babaji's Feast 121
13. The Grain-Pounder's Well 124
14. Atonement 136
15. Separation 149
16. The Pall (*Coffin*) 171

Contents

The importance of stories

'Story' has been the most important learning exercise of literature and there is the possibility that it will remain so even in the future. Every form of literature becomes the favourite form of learning among some group of literary buffs, based on their specific needs and its contemporary relevance. However, story has an evergreen and most favourite place because a story contains the element of emotion. A story does not contain useless or superfluous descriptions but has the capacity of conveying the message through implied/hidden expressions. Those emotions which cannot be very easily expressed in other forms of literature can be very effectively introduced in the deeds and words of the characters of a story. Only that story which has a good story value and earns the reader's undisturbed attention with its creative expression, dons the title of the best story!

Hindi literature has a rich tradition of story telling. Many authors have ensured with their contributions that the stories do not become outdated. No author starts writing creative stories with the intention that his story should be the best. A story becomes popular not only based on its contemporary relevance but also based on its acceptance or rejection by readers. Along with the readers, critics too play an important role in popularizing a story or making it a bestseller; thus a story just does not become popular without any effort. In fact, a story becomes special only when it has the essence of the author's soul in it.

We love Chandradhar Sharma Guleri's story '*Buddhoo ka kanta*' (The thorn of the fool) because Bhaagvanthi, the heroine of this story is a very fickle-minded and restless lady, who describes the psychological side of man-woman relationships in a very entertaining way. 'Who will swirl around her *lehanga* in front of a simpleton?' This dialogue of Bhaagvanthi, sharply brings out the essence of the story at once. The story '*Raghunath ki jhemp* '

(Raghunath's shame), is more attractive because of this character. Yashpal' story *'Nyay Aur Dhand'* (Justice and punishment) very vividly brings out all the aspects of the disparities between the haves and have-nots of the society through the character Dhakkoo Doomne, in a very harsh manner. The attack of the upper classes on Dhakkoo evokes empathy in the minds of the readers towards Dhakkoo and pushes him down to the depth of sympathy. This is the grandeur of this story. True though it is that Yashpal presents the story in a very organized manner by expressing all his thoughts through his characters, what makes the story grander and greater, is the presence of the caustic sting in the story. The creativity and the speciality of the theme only take the credit of making the stories of authors like Jynendra Agnay, Upendranath Ashk, Mohan Rakesh, Kamaleshwar and Rajendra Yadav, glorious. The same is true in case of the success of world Hindi literature as also that of Hindi fiction, in particular.

The fictions penned by the Emperor of Fictions Munshi Premchand portray his versatility and his knowledge of a variety of subjects. We can feel the pulse of the characters very clearly in their difficulties and dealings in nearly three hundred stories; countless incidents and innumerable characters! The reader gets tied down with the glimpses of reality that he is introduced to by Premchand in his wonderful mix of characterization and incidents in his stories. Premchand's linguistic style and coverage of issues are so natural and absorbing that the stories stand apart. His characters are all here and real. They are the very same as the puppets in flesh and blood that live on this earth and are endowed with the same common feelings/nature/character such as good virtues, evil traits, cleverness, selfishness, selflessness, humility etc. None of Premchand's stories is meaningless. Every story is meaningful. Every creation relates so well with the reader that it becomes great.

All stories of Premchand are special. The Indian culture gets portrayed very lustrously in them. This way, every story has abundant features that make the story unforgettable. The appropriate sentences in the story tell a lot in just a few words.

The relevance of Premchand's stories is boundless by time. There is abundant literature available about this great author but every collection has a different viewpoint and therefore, serves a different purpose. This collection has been brought out with the hope that these great stories too will evoke different kinds of interests in ordinary readers and research scholars.

Dr.Sushilkumar 'Phull'

Dr. Aashu 'Phull'.

Bade Ghar Ki Beti
(The Rich Man's Daughter)

An individual's generosity, tolerance and inherited good culture are helpful to maintain the harmony in the family. Anandi's tact in dealing with the family issues helps her succeed in beating the tensions in the family and maintaining the balance.

Benimadhav Singh was the Zamindar and Nambardar of Gowripur village. His father once used to be very affluent with a lot of wealth in cash and kind. The well built temple and pond, which remain irreparable today, were his important contributions to the village. It is said an elephant used to linger around the doorway, where today stood an old buffalo, which was a mere skeleton but probably yielded a good quantity of milk, because some one or the other stood with a pitcher by her side at all times! Benimadhav Singh had gifted more than half his wealth to lawyers. His present income did not exceed one thousand rupees per annum. The Thakur had two sons. The elder son was Shrikant Singh. He had obtained a B.A. degree after laboring and struggling for a long period of time.He was now employed in an office. The younger son Lal Bihari Singh was awell-built handsome youth. Plumpy face and broad shouldered! As soon as he woke up in the morning, he used to gobble down two *seers* (measure) of fresh buffalo milk. Shrikant Singh's plight was quite the opposite. He had sacrificed all the physical features over the two letters **B.A.**These two letters had weakened his body and drained all the glitter from his face. Therefore, he had great love for medical literature. He had more trust in Ayurvedic medicines. Day- in and day-out, one could hear the melodious rhythm of the mortar from his room. He kept corresponding regularly with the physicians of Calcutta and Lahore.

Though Shrikant possessed an English degree, he was not a great lover of the English social practices. Instead he vehemently criticized them and spurned them. This earned him great respect in his village. During Dusshera, he enthusiastically participated in the Ramlila celebrations and even adorned the role of some character or the other. He was the one who began the celebrations of Ramlila in Gowripur. The main factor of his religious belief was his appreciation of ancient Hindu civilization. He was the only devotee of the extended family. He felt that the fact that the women were losing their interest in living in undivided joint families was harmful both to the caste as well as the nation. This was the reason why the young women of the village were his calumniators. Some of them did not even hesitate to consider him as their enemy. His own wife opposed him in this matter. This was not because of her disgust against her parents-in-law or brothers-in-law. She felt that if it was not possible to manage a joint family after putting up with/giving so much of hardship of/to others, it was not worth it and it was better for each one to cook his own meal (meaning each sub-group to live separately) and avoid wasting one's entire life in infighting.

Anandi hailed from a respected upper caste family. Her father was the *Talukhedhar* of a small estate. All the known possessions of a rich and famous *Talukhedhar* were present– a huge bungalow, an elephant, three dogs, chandeliers, watch and ward staff, musical instruments, honorary title of magistrate and loans. His name was Bhoop Singh. He was very intelligent and broad-minded but unfortunately, he had no sons. He had seven daughters and by the grace of God, all of them were alive. He conducted the first three weddings very lavishly, in high spirits but then when a debt of nearly fifteen to twenty thousand fell on his head, his eyes opened and therefore, he tied his hands. Anandi was the fourth daughter. She was the most beautiful and good-natured of all. Therefore, Thakur Bhoop Singh used to love her a lot. Perhaps, there are no parents who do not love a beautiful offspring. Thakur Bhoop Singh was in a fix as to how to wed her off. He neither wished to add further to the burden of his debt nor did he want her to consider herself unlucky. One day Shrikant came to him seeking for some donation. It seemed like the donation was towards wooing the clever lady! Bhoop Singh was enamoured by his nature and Anandi was married off to Shrikant Singh in a grand manner.

When Anandi stepped into her new home, she saw a totally different picture. There were no signs of the luxuries to which she was so used to in her home right from childhood. Let alone horses and elephants, there was not even a carriage drawn by oxen! She had brought a pair of silk slippers with her but where was the garden here? There were not even windows in the house! No carpets on the floor and no hangings on the walls! This was the house of a very ordinary village family. But very soon, she adjusted herself so conveniently to the new situation that it seemed she had never ever seen any luxury in her life!

One afternoon Lal Bihari Singh came home with a couple of birds in his hands and told his sister-in-law, "Cook fast. I am hungry". Anandi had already cooked the meal and was awaiting his arrival. Now she ventured into cooking a new recipe. On checking, she found just a little ghee in the pitcher. Being from a rich family, what did she know of austerity? She poured the entire quantity of ghee over the meat. Lal Bihari Singh sat for his lunch and found no ghee in the *dal* (gravy made of pulses). He asked her, "why is there no ghee in this *dal?"*

Anandi replied, "all the ghee was used up to cook the meat".

Lal Bihari shouted, "ghee was bought just a few days ago and already its gone?"

Anandi replied, "there was hardly a *pav* (a measure) of ghee left today and I used it all up to cook the meat".

Just as a dry stick catches fire readily, a person mad with hunger, flares up over very petty issues. Lal Bihari felt very bad with this impertinence of his sister-in-law and angrily retorted, "maybe a river of ghee flows in your mom's place!"

A woman can put up with insults or even physical abuse but can never bear to hear ill of her maiden home. Anandi turned her face and said, "an elephant fetches nine lakhs even when it is dead(an idiom)! This much of ghee is eaten there by barbers and other low-caste workers everyday!"

Lal Bihari got enraged, threw his plate and said, "I feel like pulling out that tongue of yours".

Anandi too got mad, red faced, and said, "if that was possible, we could have enjoyed this episode today".

Now the uneducated and ignorant Thakur could not control himself. His wife was the daughter of an ordinary Zamindar. He raised his arm against her as and when he felt like it. He threw the wooden sandals at Anandi and said, "I will teach both you and the one, in whose arrogance you have forgotten yourself, a good lesson."

Anandi held her hands against the sandals and protected her head. But her finger was injured badly. She was palpitating out of anger like the leaves fluttering due to heavy wind. She came and stood in her room. A woman's strength, self-respect and status are limited only up to her husband. She takes pride only in the manhood and strength of her husband. Anandi swallowed blood (an idiom) and controlled herself!

Shrikant Singh used to come home on Saturdays. This episode happened on a Thursday. She remained in the den of anger during those two days. She neither drank nor ate anything and waited for his arrival. At the end, as scheduled, he returned home on time and sat outside, discussing a few mundane matters, a few matters of national importance and a few things about fresh litigations. This went on until ten in the night. The learned villagers enjoyed such discussions so much, that they could even forget their hunger. Shrikant used to find it hard to disengage himself. Anandi spent these two to three hours with much difficulty. Somehow, finally the meal time arrived! The Panchayat dispersed. Privacy prevailed and Lal Bihari said, "*Bhaiyya*, please advise sister-in-law to control her tongue while speaking, lest things may go haywire".

Benimadhav Singh supported his son and said, "Yes, it is not a right behavior of the daughters and daughters-in-law to argue with the men-folk of the family".

Lal Bihari added, "if she is from a rich family, we too are not just low-caste farmers".

Shrikant worriedly inquired, "what's the matter?"

Lal Bihari said, “nothing wrong. She herself started quarrelling just like that. She has no respect for us as compared to her maiden home”.

Shrikant finished his dinner and went to Anandi. She was sitting with a heavy heart. His majesty too was very serious. Anandi commented in a caustic voice, “you must have been satisfied now!”

Shrikant replied, “Of course, very much satisfied! But what’s the trouble that you are causing in this household these days?”

Anandi’s looks sharpened with anger and her body started getting hotter like fire, out of irritation. She said, “If I get hold of the person who has ignited you, I will scorch his face”.

Shrikant: “Why are you getting so enraged? Speak up”.

Anandi: “What should I say? This is the twist of my fate. If not, would a village urchin, who is not competent to even become a *chaprasi* (peon, who does menial labour), act so arrogantly after hitting me with sandals!”

Shrikant: “I will understand only if you tell me all that happened, clearly. I do not know anything”.

Anandi: “Your pet brother asked me to cook meat on the day before yesterday. There was just a *pav* of ghee at home. I poured all that in the meat. When he sat for lunch, he asked as to why there no ghee in the *dal.* Just for this matter, he started talking ill of my maiden home, which I could not bear. I said, this quantity of ghee would be consumed by barbers and other lowly labourers there and will not even get noticed. Just for saying this, the unscrupulous fellow threw the sandals on me. Had I not shielded my head with my hands, my head would have split. You can verify from him as to whether I said the truth or not.”

Shrikant’s eyes reddened. He said, “Things have gone thus far? How dare has this urchin become!”

Anandi started weeping, which is the nature of women, as tears always wait behind the eyelids. Shrikant was a very brave and peaceful man. He hardly got angry. Women’s tears act as the fuel to ignite the fire of anger in men. He spent the whole night turning and tossing around. He could not get a wink of sleep out of distress. Early in the morning, he went to his father and said, "*Dada*, now I cannot live in this house any more".

He had reprimanded many of his friends on many occasions for uttering such words of animosity. But unfortunately, he was forced to say those very same words with his own mouth. How easy is it to advise others!

Benimadhav Singh was shattered and asked, "Why?"

Shrikant: "Because I too care for my self-respect. Injustice and obstinacy have started ruling in this house of yours. People, who should be respecting the elders, have started pouncing on their heads. Being somebody's servant, I am away from home most of the time. In my absence, sandals and shoes are rained on my wife. Never mind about bitter words spoken! I may bear a word extra here and there but I would definitely not put up silently with blows and kicks."

Benimadhav Singh could not say a word in reply. Shrikant always respected him. Seeing this side of his son, the old Thakur was speechless. He just said, "*Beta,* being an intelligent man, are you saying such things? Women destroy homes in this manner. It is not right to pamper them so much."

Shrikant: "I understand that much. I am not so dumb, thanks to your blessings. You yourself know how many homes have been saved by my interference and advice, in this village. But I abhor this kind of evil injustice and inhuman behavior against the woman, for whose self-respect I am answerable to, in the court of God. Believe me, it is not too little for me to let Lal Bihari go unpunished."

Now Benimadhav Singh too got enraged. He could not hear such words any more. He said, "Lal Bihari is your brother. If you find him doing anything wrong, you can wring his ears but......"

Shrikant: "I do not consider Lal Bihari as my brother now".

Benimadhav Singh: "Behind a woman?"

Shrikant: "Definitely not! It is because of his unreasonable and cruel behavior".

Both of them were quiet for some time. Thakur Saheb wanted his son to cool down. But he was not ready to accept that Lal Bihari had committed any improper act. In the meanwhile, a few other gentlemen of the village gathered there in the name of enjoying a session of *hukka.* Many women of the village were happy when they heard that Shrikant had a quarrel with his father for the sake of his wife. Their souls were eager to listen to the sweet words being exchanged between the father and the son. There were certain crooked-minded people too in the village, who were burning within, of jealousy about the legal status of this caste! Those people used to say, "Shrikant is scared of his father; therefore, he is a coward. He is educated and hence a mere book-worm. It is foolishness on the part of Benimadhav Singh that he does not do anything without consulting Shrikant." Today all the wishes of these great men were getting fulfilled. Some came on the pretext of smoking *hukka*, while some came on the pretext of presenting the tax receipts. Benimadhav Singh was a traditional person. He conceived their intentions. He decided that he would not give these betrayers a chance to laugh at them. Immediately, he politely said, "I am with you. Do as you like. After all the boy has erred."

The experienced and angry graduate of Allahabad could not understand this. He was used sticking to his point stubbornly in debating clubs but what did he know of such tactfulness? He did not understand the purpose behind his father turning the plate all of a sudden. He said, "I cannot live with Lal Bihari in this house anymore".

Benimadhav: "*Beta,* intelligent people do not care what the foolish people utter. He is an immature boy. Being elder to him, pardon him for his misdeeds."

Shrikant: "I cannot bear with this misdeed of his. Either he stays or I stay in this house. If he is more beloved to you, please see me off. I can take care of myself. If you want me to stay with you, tell him he can go anywhere he pleases. That's it. This is my final decision."

Lal Bihari Singh was standing silently at the doorway and listening to what his elder brother was saying. He respected him a lot. He never dared to sit on the cot or smoke *hukka* or chew *pan* in his presence. He did not respect even his father to that extent. Shrikant too was very intimate to Lal Bihari. He had never consciously ever uttered even a word against him. Whenever he came from Allahabad, he definitely brought something or the other for him. It was he, who had specially got a pair of clubs made for him (used in body building). Last year, when he defeated a contestant, who was one and half times his size, in a duel of wrestling, he felt very elated, went right inside the ring, hugged him and treated him generously with five rupees. He felt very sad to hear such heart-rending words from such a brother today. He broke down and started crying. There was no doubt he was repenting for his act. A day before his brother's arrival, he was getting nervous as to how he might react. He was wondering, 'how will I face him; how will I talk to him and how will I even raise my eyes towards him.' He had thought his brother would call him and advise. On the contrary, he found him to be a merciless idol. He was a fool. In the heart of heart he felt his brother was doing injustice to him. He would not have felt this sad if his brother had reprimanded him or even slapped him in privacy but he was unable to bear his brother not even willing to look at him. He came home crying. He went into his room, got dressed up and wiped his face so that nobody could tell that he had cried. He then went to Anandi's room, stood at the doorway and said, "*Bhabhi,* my brother has decided that he will not live with me in this house anymore. He does not want to look at my face. Therefore, I am leaving now. I will never ever show my face to him. I apologise for whatever wrong I committed. Please pardon me."

He was choking as he uttered these words.

Just when Lal Bihari Singh stood submissively at Anandi's doorway, Shrikant too came in with red eyes. No sooner he saw his brother standing, he turned his eyes with disgust and left abruptly. It seemed like he wanted to avoid even his shadow.

Anandi did complain about Lal Bihari to her husband but in the heart of heart, she was now repenting. She was compassionate and large hearted by nature. She did not have an inkling that this matter would blow up to such an extent. She was getting irritated within herself as to why her husband was getting so heated up. She was now fearing, 'what if he now beckons her to go along with him to Allahabad. What would I say to him?' In the meanwhile, when she heard the words, "I will leave. I apologise for whatever wrong I committed. Please pardon me" from Lal Bihari at her doorway, her heart melted and even the little anger that was left in her watered down. She started crying. Tears are the best cleansers to wipe away the filth in one's mind.

She saw Shrikant and said, "Lala is standing outside and weeping profusely."

Shrikant: "So, what should I do?"

Anandi: "Call him in. Let my tongue be burnt (an idiom)! Why at all did I begin this quarrel?"

Shrikant: "I will not call him."

Anandi: "You will repent. He is very hurt. Let not he really leave!"

Shrikant got up. Just then Lal Bihari repeated, "*Bhabhi,* convey my regards to *Bhaiyya.* He does not like to look at me. So, I will not show my face to him."

After saying so, Lal Bihari turned towards the main door. In the end Anandi came out of her room and held his hand. Lal Bihari turned towards her and with welled up eyes said, "Please let me go."

Anandi: "Where are you going?"

Lal Bihari: "To a place where nobody can see my face".

Anandi: "I will not let you go."

Lal Bihari: "I am not fit to live with you people."

Anandi: "I swear! You shall not take even a step forward!"

Lal Bihari: "Until I am convinced that *Bhaiyya* has nothing against me in his mind, I shall not stay here at any cost."

Anandi: "I swear upon God that I have no ill feeling whatsoever in my mind against you for sure."

Now Shrikant's heart too melted. He came out and embraced Lal Bihari. Both of them wept bitterly. With hiccups, Lal Bihari said, "*Bhaiyya*, don't ever say 'I will not look at your face'. Instead, I will gladly accept whatever punishment you give."

Shrikant replied in a choking voice, "Lallu, forget these words forever. God forbid, let such a situation not arise in the future".

Benimadhav Singh was coming from outside. He felt excited with happiness, seeing the brothers embracing each other. He said, "This is how daughters of great households are! They can mend things which may break!"

Whoever heard about this episode in the village, appreciated Anandi's compassion with the same words, "This is how daughters of great households indeed are!"

The Salt Inspector

In a system rampant with corruption, there can still be present an honest Constable like Banshidhar, who rejected promotion and found satisfaction in carrying out his duties.

When a department of 'Salt' was founded and a ban was brought against dealings in this all-important God-gifted ingredient, people started carrying on their business stealthily. Various dubious ways were found; while some found their ways by feeding bribes, others got their ways in a cunning and smart manner. The officials were flourishing. They were queuing up at the doors of this department, giving up even prestigious posts of village accountants. Even advocates craved to take up the post of an ordinary *Daroga* (Inspector) in this department.

It was a time when people thought that English education and Christianity were one and the same. Parsees were very powerful then. After reading romantic stories and literature rich in the amorous pleasures, they were getting appointed to many top posts.

Munshi Banshidhar had just started looking out for a livelihood, after completing the story of estrangement by Zulekha and considering the love affair of Seereen and Farhad more important than the epic war between Nala and Neela (the mythological monkey characters of the epic Ramayana) and the discovery of America!

His father was an experienced man. He explained, "*Beta,* you are seeing the sorry state of this house. We are sinking with the burden of debt. The girls are growing up fast like grass and weeds. I am becoming like a tree on the edge of a precipice and I do not know when I am going to fall flat! Now you are the owner-caretaker of this house.

"Don't give attention towards official ranks and positions. They are only tombs of troubles (An idiom)! Your attention should be towards mantles and offerings (An idiom)! Look out for a job where you get some extra income. Monthly income is like a full moon, which seems full only on one day and wanes away day by day. But extra earnings are like a perennial stream, which quenches the thirst forever. Salary is given by man, but nobody progresses only with that. Extra earnings are gifted by God and those are what bring prosperity to a person. You yourself are a scholar and why should I be explaining all this to you!

One needs great wisdom in this matter. Look at a man, look at his needs and look at the opportunities and then decide whatever you feel is the best! It is most beneficial to act strict with people in need. But it is a difficult proposition to deal with a man who has no needs. Remember these words forever; they are my life's earnings!"

With this advice, the father blessed the son. Banshidhar was an obedient son. He listened to the advice very attentively and then left home. In this wide world, courage was his friend, profession was his guide and self-dependence was his assistant. But seemed like he had left at the most auspicious moment! Therefore, he got appointed as the Inspector in the Salt Department. The salary was good and there was unlimited scope for extra earnings. When old Munshiji heard about this news, his joy knew no bound! The money-lenders softened their stand, the toddy merchants' creeper of aspirations for good business was green with fresh leavesand neighbours' hearts were feeling the pain of jealousy!

It was winter and night time. The soldiers and guards of the Salt Department were intoxicated. It was just a few months since Banshidhar had joined duty but within that limited time, he had won the hearts of his superior officers with his skill and good conduct. Officers started trusting him a lot.

At a distance of about a mile to the east of the Salt Department, flowed Jamuna river and there was a bridge of boats across the river. The Inspector locked the door and was enjoying a good sleep. Suddenly he awoke with the rumbling noise of carts and the chattering voices of the boatmen instead of the noise of the flowing water. He sat up.

Why are carts going towards the river at this unearthly hour? Definitely there is something fishy. His intellect clarified his imagination. He wore his uniform, kept his revolver in his pocket and within no time set off towards the bridge on his horse. He reached the spot. He saw a caravan of carts proceeding towards the bridge. He inquiredharshly, "whose carts are these?"

There was silence for some time. The men whispered something amongst themselves and then one of them said, "they belong to Pandit Alopeedeen".

"Who is Pandit Alopeedeen?"

"He is from Datagunj".

Munshi Banshidhar was shocked. Pandit Alopeedeen was the most powerful *Jamindar* of that region. He dealt in lakhs of rupees. There was none, from the ordinary to the rich, of this region who was not indebted to him. He had a huge business. The *Jamindar*was a very clever man. English officers came to his region for hunting and stayed as his guests. There were parties all the year round.

Munshi asked, "where are the carts going to?"

"Kanpur", came the reply.

But when he questioned as to what the carts contained, there was silence. The Inspector's suspicion grew.

After waiting for a reply for sometime, he questioned, "Have you all gone dumb? I am asking what is loaded in these carts?"

When he got no answer even this time, he proceeded near a cart on his horse and groped a loaded sack. His doubt got cleared. Those were bags of salt.

Pandit Alopeedeen was coming in his decorated carriage, half asleep. All of a sudden, many bewildered cart-men came to him and woke him up saying, "*Maharaj*, the Inspector has stopped the carts and is asking you to go to the jetty.

Pandit Alopeedeen had unlimited trust in Goddess Lakshmi. He often used to say, 'what to say of this world, even heaven is under Lakshmi's rule.' It was quite natural of him to say so. Justice and law were all Lakshmi's toys and she could play with them as she pleased. Lying down, he proudly said, "okay. I will come". Saying so, he prepared a *beeda* out of *pan* leaves and started chewing it, with least worry. Then he approached the *daroga*, wrapping himself in a shawl and said, "*Babuji,* blessings! Please tell me as to what crime has been committed by us that you have stopped my carts. Your kind attention towards us Brahmins should always prevail."

Banshidhar sternly said, "Government order."

Pandit Alopeedeen laughed and said, "I neither know Government orders nor the Government. You are my Government. The relationship between you and me is a domestic relationship; how can I become an outsider all of a sudden? You have taken unnecessary trouble. It can never happen that we pass by this side and never contribute our offerings to the God on this bank. I was in fact on my way to personally come and meet you."

The enchantress of wealth could not influence Banshidhar in any way. There was a new ecstasy in honesty. He replied in a strong tone, "I am not amongst those betrayers, who roam around selling away their honesty just for a few pennies. You are now under arrest. I will draw a challan as per rules. I have no time for wasting on unnecessary talk. *Jamadaar* Badloo Singh! You take him into custody and go along. This is my order."

Pandit Alopeedeen was stunned. There was unrest among the cartmen. This was the first time in the life of Pandit, that he had to hear such strong words. Badloo Singh advanced but out of reverence, he did not get the courage to hold Panditji by hand. Panditji had never seen virtue disrespecting wealth to this extent. He thought that this boy was really arrogant. He is yet to fall into the trap of glamour and allurement. He is inexperienced and therefore acting smart. He said, in a submissive tone, "*Babu Saheb,* please don't do this. We will be ruined. Our image will be spoilt. By insulting me, what do you get? In whichever way we see, I am no stranger to you."

Banshidhar sternly said, "I do not want to hear such words."

The same cliff that he thought was a great support to him was now giving away below his feet. His self respect and his wealth received a great blow. But he still had trust in the strength of the bountiful wealth. He told his deputy, "Lalaji, gift a note of one thousand to Babu Saheb; he is becoming a hungry Singh at present".

Banshidhar turned red with anger and said, "A thousand or even a lakh will not tempt me away from the right path."

Panditji got irritated with the stupid stubbornness of virtue and a sacrifice that cannot even please God. Now there was a tussle between both the strengths. Wealth started attacking with more and more vigour. From one to five, five to ten, ten to fifteen and fifteen to it reached even twenty! But the strong virtue of honesty stood undisturbed with a supernatural bravery all alone like a great mountain facing the large army of wealth.

Alopeedeen was disappointed and said, "I cannot go any further. Now, it is left to your power".

Banshidhar called out to his *Jamadhaar.* Badloo Singh, cursing the *Daroga* in his mind, advanced towards Panditji. Panditji stepped back a little with fear. He very submissively said, "Babu Saheb, please show mercy on me for God's sake. I am ready to settle for twenty five thousand."

"Impossible".

"Thirty thousand?"

"Impossible at any cost".

"What, not even for forty thousand?"

"Not possible for forty thousand or even a forty lakh."

"Badloo Singh, take this man into custody. I do not want to hear even a single word".

Honesty defeated wealth fully. Alopeedeen saw a hefty person proceeding towards him with handcuffs. He looked around with disappointment and despair. He then fell down unconscious.

The world was asleep but the tongues were wide awake. In the morning, this matter was heard from everybody's mouth right from a child to an old person. Everybody was seen analyzing and criticizing Panditji's act in detail and showering insults on him, as though this was the last act of dishonesty on this earth.

The cowherd who was selling water in the name of milk, the officials who were maintaining fake records, the *babus* who were travelling ticketless in trains, the *Seth* who wascreating fake documents were also joining the above, as if they were Gods.

On the next day, as Pandit Alopeedeen was walking as an accused along with the constables, in handcuffs, with a heavy heart, bending down his head out of shame towards the court, there was unrest in the entire town. Even a fair would not have been such a feast to the expectant eyes! The roofs and walls were overflowing with crowds and two could never be distinguished.

There was still time for Panditji to arrive at the court. Pandit Alopeedeen was the lion of this huge forest. Officials were his worshippers, administrative staff members were his workers, lawyers and their deputies were his obedient followers, orderlies, peons and watchmen were his free slaves!

On seeing him, people were running from all sides. Everybody was surprised not because Alopeedeen had committed this act but as to how he got himself caught in the claws of law. How can such a man who had wealth that could achieve impossible things and who was no match for anyone in his smart-talk, come into the claws of law? Everybody was showing his sympathy to him.

An army of advocates was formed with great care and urgency, to prevent this attack. A war broke out between honesty and wealth in the field of justice. Banshidhar stood silently. He had no strength other than truth and clear expression was his only weapon. There were witnesses but all of them were swaying out of greed.

Munshiji felt even justice was being dragged to his side unnaturally. It was the *durbar* of justice but the employees were all intoxicated with an attitude of bias. What is the union of justice and partiality? Where there is a biased approach, we cannot even imagine that justice will prevail. The case was settled very soon.

The Deputy Magistrate wrote in his judgement that the complaint given against Pandit Alopeedeen was baseless and imaginary. He is a very wealthy figure. It is unimaginable that he would have dared to commit such an act just for the sake of a few pennies. It was not a very grave mistake on the part of Munshiji; however because of his arrogance and shortsightedness, a good person had to undergo such an insulting experience. The Magistrate further stated, 'Though we are pleased that the *Daroga* is vigilant and ever-cautious in his job but his loyalty to the law exaggerated by this case, has blinded his intellect and wisdom. He has to be more careful in future.'

The advocates were thrilled hearing this judgement. Pandit Alopeedeen came out of the court with a smile. His family and friends celebrated lavishly. A sea of benevolence roared. Its waves shook the very foundation of the court.

When Banshidhar came out of the court, sharp arrows of sarcasm were rained on him. *Chaprasis* saluted him with bent heads. But at that moment every harsh comment and every look aroused the fire of pride in him.

Of course he was not walking proudly after winning this case. But he had a very sad and strange experience about this world. Nothing deserved true respect – the law and knowledge, lengthy titles, long beards or the long gowns- nothing in fact!

Banshidhar had won the enmity of wealth and he had to pay for it. Just a week had passed with difficulty, when his suspension order arrived! He got punished for his devotion to duty. The poor man went home with a heavy heart filled with deep sorrow. Old Munshiji had already started fuming, 'this boy did not listen to any word of caution that I gave him before he left. He does as he pleases. I put up with all the demands of the toddy-seller and butcher and am now sitting as a helpless devotee in my old age and just a petty salary there?! I have also worked but was not a big officer. But used to work, work whole-heartedly and you tried to be great torchbearer of honesty! The house may be in the dark, we shall light lamps at the Masjid without fail! I pity on such an understanding! All the education gone down the drain!'

Just after a few days, when Munshi Banshidhar returned home in a bad shape and broke the news to his old father, he lamented and said, "I feel like smashing both your head and mine." For long time he kept wringing his hands in repentance. He even uttered a few harsh words to himand the scene would have turned ugly, had Banshidhar not left the spot. The old mother too was very upset.Her aspirations to go on a pilgrimage to Jagannath Temple and Rameshwaram were shattered. Banshidhar's wife did not even speak to him properly for a long time.

One week passed by this way. It was evening time. Old Munshiji was sitting and chanting the name Ram, with a rosary in his hands. Just then a decorated carriage stopped at his door. Green and pink curtains, a pair of oxen of foreign breed, with blue thread around their necks and horns clad in shining brass! There were many workers with *lathis* accompanying the carriage.

Munshiji went out to check on the visitors and found Pandit Alopeedeen! He bowed down with respect and started flattering him, "It is our good fortune that you have graced our doorstep. You are our respectful God! How to show my stained face to you? What can I do? My son turned out to be a wretched disloyal son. Otherwise would such a situation arise where I have to hide my face from you? It would have been better even if God had not blessed me with children instead of giving me such a son."

Alopeedeen said, "No, no *Bhai Saheb,* don't say such things."

Munshiji replied with a surprise, "What else can I say with such a son?"

Alopeedeen said in a loving tone, "How many honest sons would you find in this world, who would sacrifice everything to uphold truth and honesty and bring laurel to their families and ancestors?"

Pandit Alopeedeen said to Banshidhar, "*Darogaji,* please do not take this as flattery. I need not have taken so much trouble to come and flatter you. That night you took me into your custody with the help of your official power, but today I have willingly come into your custody. I have seen thousands of rich and powerful people and dealt with thousands of top officials, but you are the one who dethroned me. I made everyone slaves to myself and my wealth. Please permit me to entreat you".

Banshidhar got up and welcomed Alopeedeen when he came, but with self-respect. He thought that this man has come to insult him and burn him down. He never made any attempt to seek pardon. His father's flattery disgusted him. When he heard Panditji's words, the ill-feelings in his heart vanished.

He looked at Panditji with raised head. Warmth could be felt in his eyes. Pride submitted before shame. He said shyly, "It is your generosity that you are saying this. Please pardon me for my impertinence. I was tied down by the shackles of honesty lest I am your slave. I will abide by your orders."

Alopeedeen said with humility, "you did not heed to my prayer at the Ghat, but today you ought to accept."

Banshidhar said, "Of what use am I? But there will be no compromise in whatever service that I can do for you."

Alopeedeen placed a stamped document in front of him and said, "Please accept this post and sign on this document. I am a Brahmin and I will not move out of your doorstep until and unless you fulfill this prayer of mine."

When Munshi Banshidhar read the document, his eyes welled-up with tears of gratitude. Pandit Alopeedeen had appointed him as the Permanent Manager of his entire property- six thousand rupees of annual salary besides daily allowance, a horse for conveyance, a residential bungalow with the free service of servants and attendants. Munshi said in a trembling voice, "Panditji, I am not capable enough to appreciate your generosity but I am not fit for such a high post."

Alopeedeen laughed and said, "at present I need only an unfit person."

Banshidhar replied majestically, " I remain your servant. It is my good fortune to serve a famous and respectable person like you. But I do not have the required qualification and knowledge. Neither do I have the nature that can compensate lack of these. A very experienced and knowledgeable person can only suit such a great post."

Alopeedeen removed a pen from the pen-holder and handed it over to Banshidhar, saying, "I do not desire qualification or experience or knowledge or skill. I have realized the value of these qualities very well. Luckily for me, destiny has gifted me with that gem whose radiance has dimmed the brilliance of suitability and qualification. Take this pen and without thinking too much, sign the papers. I pray to the God that you remain the same needless, arrogant, strict but honest *Daroga* whom I met on the Ghat."

Banshidhar's eyes was wet with tears. He could not contain that much of gratitude in the limited space of his heart. He looked at Panditji once again with devotion and respect and signed on the papers with his shivering hand.

Alopeedeen was very happy and embraced Banshidhar.

The Two Brothers

Jealousy and enmity can bring rifts even between two natural brothers. One brother takes advantage of his brother's helplessness and loots his wealth. This story is a straight blow on greed at its peak!

Early in the morning, Kalavathi was feeding *roti* and milk to her two children, who were sitting on her lap, enjoying the beautiful and soothing rays of the rising sun. Kedar was the elder son, while Madhav the younger one. Both of them would fill their mouths with morsel of food each, jump around a few steps and come back to her lap once again, repeating a prayer in their baby-talk. The prayer was written by a kind-hearted poet, who was expressing the suffering of a young lad shivering in cold winter, in a heart-rending way:

Oh God! Warm up your child, he is very cold!

The mother beckoned them fondly and fed them bigger and bigger morsels each time. Her heart was filled with love and her eyes shone with pride. Both the brothers grew up. They used to hug each other and play together. Kedar had a sharp intellect, while Madhav was physically strong. Both of them were so friendly that they would go to school together, eat together and stay together. Both of them got married. Kedar's wife Champa was talkative and restless. Madhav's wife Shyama was of dark complexion, beautiful and a treasure-house of good looks. She was very soft-spoken, well-behaved and peaceful.

Kedar was attracted towards Champa, while Madhav was very satisfied with Shyama. But Kalavathi could not get along with both of them. She was equally happy and unhappy about both of them. The major part of her training focused on her efforts to see that at least a little of Champa's skills could be exchanged for Shyama's peaceful nature but all her efforts went in vain.

Both the brothers had children. The lush green tree branched around generously and yielded loads of fruits, while the fragile tree yielded just one fruit, that too a weak and pale one. Yet both the brothers were unhappy. While Madhav was greedy of wealth, Kedar was aspiring to have children!

The crookedness of fate gradually turned into enmity, which was but only natural. Shyama was ever busy tending her children- dressing them up, getting them ready, etc., and had no time to even lift her head. Poor Champa ended up drowning with the burden of the kitchen chores all alone. This injustice got expressed in harsh words once in a way. Shyama just listened, lamented and put up with everything silently. But this tolerance of Shyama only increased Champa's anger, instead of cooling her down. It reached its limit when the cup of tolerance was filled to the brim! The deer, finding no way to escape, pounced on the hunter! Champa and Shyama started moving away from each other in perpendicular directions. A day arrived when two hearths started burning in the house but both the brothers did not dare eat anything and Kalavathi kept weeping all day.

Many years passed by. It became difficult for the brothers who would always sit on the same lap, eat from a common plate and drink milk from the same breast, to now live under a common roof in the same village! Just to save the image of the family, wasteful attempts were made to hide the fire of jealousy and enmity beneath its ashes! There was no brotherly attachment left in the two of them. There was just a shameful façade in the name of brotherhood! The mother was still alive and she shed tears at the enmity between her sons. She had love in her heart but her eyes did not exhibit pride. The flower was the same but it had lost its fragrance!

When the two were young lads, when one of them cried, the other too would start crying looking at him, as they were innocent, simple and ignorant. But today, when one of them cries, the other one laughs at him and rejoices. They have now become knowledgeable and intelligent!

When they had no knowledge of the distinction between their own people and strangers, if somebody teased them saying that he would take one of them along, the other one would lie down on the floor and hold that person's *Kurta.* But now even if one of them meets death, there will be no tears in the eyes of the other. Now, they were well aware of their own people and strangers!

Poor Madhav's situation was very worrisome. His expenses were more but income was limited. Over that was the burden of managing the honour of the family! Lips had to keep smiling even if the heart cried! Even if his heart had stains, his clothes should look clean! He had four sons and four daughters and the cost of necessities was too dear. How long can a few pennies manage the show? Getting sons married was at his discretion but how could he postpone getting his daughters married off? A portion of his limited landholding was gifted away during his first daughter's marriage. Despite that, the groom's family returned without even accepting his feast. The rest of his land was parted with during his second daughter's marriage. After a year, when his third daughter was married off, nothing was left. Yes. Even now the branch was lush green. But the relationship between poverty and trusteeship is like that between meat and dog!

This girl was not even sent off to her husband's house when Madhav received a warrant for payment of the arrears of tax for two years. The bride's jewellery were pledged. Champa was waiting for this opportunity only! She immediately sent words to the new relatives. "You people are sitting senselessly. Here the jewellery is vanishing". On the second day a barber and two Brahmins came and sat at the doors of Madhav. Poor Madhav felt squeezed. From where could he get money? He had no land, no property, no farm or no garden. All he had was faith, which too had departed long ago. All he had now were those two rooms, where he had spent all his life and there was no buyer for those rooms. He was getting ashamed by the delay. He became helpless, went to Kedar and with tears in his eyes said, "*Bhaiyya,* I am in deep trouble now. Please help me."

Kedar replied, "These days I am also fed up. I am telling you the truth."

Champa said in a commanding voice, “Arre! Are you getting fed up of this man too? By cooking separately, does honour too get divided?”

Kedar winked at the lady sideways and said, “no, no, I didn’t mean that. What if my hands are fed up? Definitely, some arrangement can be made.”

Champa asked Madhav, “Did you not pledge jewellery worth over hundred?”

Madhav replied, “Including interest, it must be around hundred and twenty five.”

Kedar was reading Ramayan. He started reading once again. Champa started talking philosophically, “that is big money! It was okay if we had that kind of money. But we have to get money from somebody else. A money-lender will not agree to lend the huge sum without any document.”

Madhav thought, ‘If I had property to mortgage, would I have come to you? Are there no other money lenders?’ and said, “what else is left with me? All I have now is this house.”

Kedar and Champa looked at each other understandingly and thought within their minds, ‘are our fervent desires going to be truly met today?’ But by the time their thought came to their tongue, it took a decent form. Champa very seriously said, “No money lender would ever lend against this house! Had it been in a city, it may earn some rent. But being in a village, no one would occupy the house, even if given free. It is just a piece of decoration.”

Kedar feared that their plans may get defunct by Champa’s harsh approach. He said, “I do know a particular money-lender. He might probably listen to me.”

Champa shook her head in appreciation of Kedar’s ploy and said, “But it may not fetch more than around sixty.”

Kedar boldly took a risk and said, “by pressurizing a bit more, it may go up to eighty. What else?”

Champa looked seriously at Kedar and said with dissatisfaction, “A money-lender is not this blind”.

Madhav could, to some extent, understand the secret plan of his brother and sister-in-law. He was surprised as to from where the two of them gained such cleverness. He asked, "where can I get the balance amount?"

Champa said with irritation, "Think more about the balance amount. These two rooms will definitely not fetch hundred and twenty five. We can get you upto eighty from a money-lender. Prepare the document".

Madhav became suspicious with this secretive plan. He felt the two of them were into some deep conspiracy against him. He stood to his point and said, "what more to think about? If we had jewels, I would have pledged them. We don't even have plain cloth. When I am defamed, how does it matter whether I lose my face for a ten or a fifty! It all means the same. If I can save my image by selling the house it's fine; but I am not prepared for a proposal where I lose my house and still lose my face. If it was just for the sake of saving my name, what can anybody do if I am not interested in saving it? To tell you the truth, I am least bothered about my name. Who knows me? My brother will become a laughing stock."

Kedar's face lost its glitter. Champa too was shaken. She was very smart in her talks. She did not expect such a strong attitude from a simpleton Madhav. She looked at him with respect and said, "Lalu, some times you too talk like a child! Who will grant a hundred against this hut? Enough if you get a hundred only if not hundred and twenty five! I will also sell my share right today. Isn't my share too the same? You can get only one hundred against the house. You and I shall make other arrangements for the rest of the money. Honour is of both of us and we shall not lose it. The money shall be accounted for separately."

Madhav's wishes were fulfilled. He achieved his goal. He thought, 'all I need is money. How does it matter whether is accounted in one account or ten accounts! And as far as the house is concerned, I am not going to quit until I die. He went back happily. Long after he left, Kedar and Champa gave up their farcical façade and kept blaming each other for the unfavourable decision that they had taken. In the end, they convinced themselves that though the feast was not very tasty, after all it was filling! And the house! 'Let's see how Shyama Rani is going to rule in this house!'

Two bullocks stood at the doors of Kedar. There was so much of love, friendliness and unity between the two of them. Both of them carry a common yoke. That's all is the relationship between the two. Even then, when one of them had gone to Champa's maiden home for an engagement, the other one did not eat anything for three days. But it is sad that the brothers who played on the same lap and suckled the same breast today have become such strangers to each other that they do not like to even live under a common roof.

It was early morning. The village chief and accountant arrived at the house of Kedar. Munshi Datadayal Abhiman sat on the cot, preparing the mortgage documents. He kept dipping the pen in the ink and writing the deed but the deed did not look any better. Kedar's face bloomed up and Champa could not contain her excitement. Madhav was pale and glum.

The village chief said, "A brother has to be as supportive as this and not an enemy. Kedar has saved the image of his brother."

The Accountant agreed, "A brother indeed should be like this."

The assistant of the accountant said, "*Bhai,* this is the duty of dutiful sons."

Datadayal asked, "Name of the mortgager?"

The elder brother said, "Madhav Vald Shivadutt".

"And the mortgagee?"

"Kedar Vald Shivadutt."

Madhav looked at his elder brother with a shock. His eyes welled up with tears. Kedar could not look at Madhav directly. The village chief, accountant and his assistant were all surprised. Is Kedar himself lending the money? But actually it seemed like some money-lender was to be a party to this deed. When the money is very much available at home, what was the need for this mortgage deed? So much of distrust between brothers?! Arre! Ram! Ram! Is Madhav not even worth 80 rupees? In case Madhav did default, would the money flow wastefully in the waters?

All the eyes were communicating in sign language and it seemed as though boats were swaying away in the deep river of surprise.

Shyama was standing at the entrance. She always praised Kedar but today only social etiquette stopped her from raising her arm against her husband's elder brother.

When the old mother heard about his, the dry river got alive. She looked at the sky and beat her forehead with her palm.

She recollected how on one such beautiful morning, two lovely children played on her lap, eating *roti* and drinking milk. At that time the mother was full of pride and her heart was filled with hope and enthusiasm.

But today.....Ah! Today her eyes were filled with shame and her heart was heavy with sorrow and grief. She looked at the earth and said, "Hey Narayan (taking the name of the Almighty Narayan)! Should I have given birth to such children?"

Pancha Parameshwar
(Parameshwar the Arbitrator)

It is believed that the Paramatma (supreme soul) resides in Arbitrators. The one who occupies the seat of an arbitrator is neither a friend nor a foe to anyone. It is before him that the truth prevails (the water in the milk gets exposed). This is an ideal story woven of taunts and reproach.

There was intense friendship between Jumman Sheikh and Alagu Chaudhary. There were some give and take transactions between the two. The two of them trusted each other thoroughly. When Jumman went on Haj, he had entrusted his house to Alagu and likewise whenever Alagu went out of station, he left his house in the care of Jumman. They never ate together or followed a common religion. But their ideologies were the same. That is what is the strength of friendship.

This friendship bloomed right from their childhood when Jumman's father Jumrathi used to teach both of them. Alagu served his Guruji (teacher) very sincerely, washing his clothes and vessels on many occasions. His *hookah* never rested even for a while because Alagu used to be off his books for nearly half an hour every time to light it! Alagu's father was an old-fashioned man. He trusted more on the service of Guru than on education. He used to say that nobody gains knowledge by reading but only with the blessings of a Guru. It is enough if one has the Guru's kind attention. Just in case Alagu did not gain much by Jumrathi's blessings and his association, he would convince himself presuming that Alagu had not put in his full efforts for gaining knowledge and if he is not at all fated to be knowledgeable, how could he gain knowledge?

But Jumrathi himself was not convinced about his blessings. He trusted his weapon of words more than anything and today only on account of the influence of that weapon, Jumman was being worshipped not only in his village but even in the neighbouring villages. No official could point out any error in the mortgage deeds or documents drafted by him. The area postman, constable and the peon of the *Tehsil* (Collector's office)- all of them aspired for his grace. Thus wealth earned Alagu fame, while Jumman Sheikh earned the respect of all because of his rich knowledge.

Jumman Sheikh had an old aunt. She had a little wealth but she had no relatives around her. Jumman somehow got that wealth bequeathed to himself by arguing a lot with her. Until the gift deed was registered, the aunt was highly respected and treated well. She was fed with the best food. There was a rain of *halwa* and *pullav*! But once the gift deed was stamped, it seemed the stamp was also affixed on these hospitalities! Jumman's wife Kareeman started serving the old lady with a little of sharp and intense taunts seasoned with her bitter tongue along with *roties.* Jumman Sheikh too turned heartless. Now the poor aunt had to bear these sharp taunts all through the day.

Nobody knew how long the old lady would live. Having given just a few yards of dry land, does she think he has earned a great wealth? She does not relish *roties* with a tasty *dal!* With the money spent on feeding this old woman, he could have bought the entire village!

For a few days the aunt bore all the insults silently but when things went too far and she could bear no more, she complained to Jumman. Jumman did not find it appropriate to interfere in the system established by the domestic employee – homemaker! Things moved on with the same complaints. In the end, the aunt told Jumman one day, "I cannot live with you anymore. Please give me some money and I shall cook my food on my own."

Jumman replied audaciously, "does money grow on trees here?"

The aunt said politely, "Don't I need at least some food to survive?"

Jumman replied seriously, "Did anybody think that you have defeated mortality?"

The aunt got enraged. She threatened him of calling for a Panchayat. Jumman laughed just as a hunter laughs within himself seeing his prey (a deer) advancing towards the net prepared by him! He said, "Oh, yes! Please do convene a Panchayat. Let the matter get settled. I too am fed with this irritation day and night."

Jumman had no doubt as to who would win in the Panchayat. Who was not obliged to him in all the neighbouring villages and who had the guts to win his enmity? Who had the strength to face him? The angels will not land from the sky to hold the Panchayat!

After this, the old woman kept roaming around all the nearby villages with a walking stick. Her back had sunk and bent fully. Every step was a great struggle but the matter had arisen and something had to be decided.

There were but a few good men before whom she had not shed her tears of remorse. Some of them brushed aside her woes with a few words of lip sympathy while some of them blamed the times for this great injustice. They said, "you have one foot in the grave but still your thirst is not quenched. What do you want now? Eat *roties* and chant the name of Allah. What do you have to do with farming now?" There were certain other good people, who got an opportunity to enjoy a bit of comedy. Why wouldn't they laugh at the character whose back was bent, face was wrinkled and toothless and hair was knotted? There were very few just, generous, compassionate and loving men who listened to the orphan woman's sob story seriously and sympathized her. After roaming around all the directions, she reached Alagu Choudhary. She dropped her *lathi* and said, after heaving a sigh, "Son, you too attend my Panchayat for a few minutes."

Alagu: "what is the use of inviting me? There will be so many others from all the villages."

Aunt: "I have cried out my heart before everybody. It is left to them whether to attend or not."

Alagu: "I can come just for the sake of coming. But I will not open my mouth in the Panchayat."

Aunt: "Why,my son?"

Alagu: "What can I say for this? It's my wish. Jumman is my old friend. I do not want to spoil our relationship."

Aunt: "Son, will you not even speak the truth in the fear of breaking your friendship?"

Our dormant sense of honesty/truthfulness will not even be realized when it is looted entirely. But it will get aroused once it is challenged! Then nobody can defeat it. Alagu could not give any answer to the old woman's question but it kept ringing in his mind – 'what? Will you not even speak the truth in the fear of breaking your friendship?'

In the evening, the Panchayat was convened under a tree. Sheikh Jumman had already spread a cushioned bed-sheet on the floor. He had organized for *Pan, ilaychi* (cardamom), *Hookah-thambaku* (tobacco), etc. He deliberately sat at a decent distance from Alagu Choudhary. Whenever anybody entered the Panchayat, he wished them bowing down his head. When the sun set and the Panchayat of the chirping birds convened noisily on the tree, the Panchayat meet below the tree. The spread was full of people, but most of them were silent audience. Out of the invitees, only those of them who had some reason to settle their scores with Jumman were present at the Panchayat. In one corner there was a kindling ember, from which the barber was lighting the *Hookah* pot. It was difficult to say whether the smoke emitted by the pot of tobacco was more or that emitted by the burning fuel of dried cow-dung cake. Boys were running hither and thither. Some of them were spurning insults at each other, while some of them were weeping. There was pow-wow all around. The village dogs mistook this for a gathering of feast and hence gathered there in packs.

As soon as the Panchayat arbitrators took their seat, the old aunt presented her case-

"Sirs, it's been three years since I transferred all my property in the name of my nephew. Indeed all of you know about this. Jumman had then agreed to provide me food and clothing for life. Somehow I spent these years begging and lamenting. But now I am unable to bear the pain of crying day and night. I neither get fed fully nor clothed properly. I am a helpless widow. I cannot run around courts and police stations. Other than you, where else can I go and cry out my woes? I will follow the path that you lay. If you find any wrong in me, slap me. If you find some shortcoming in Jumman, please advise him as to why he is torturing a helpless widow. I will obey the orders of this Panchayat dutifully."

Ramdhan Mishra, whose many tenants had been lured by Jumman and settled in his village, said, "My friend Jumman, whom do you want to nominate as the *Panch?* Settle the issue right now. If not, you will be forced to follow whatever the Panchayat decides."

Jumman could spot only such people with whom he had differences for some reason or the other sitting as Panchayat members. Jummman said, "the orders of the Panchayat members are those of the Allah. Let *Khalajaan* (aunt) nominate anybody she wishes. I have no problem."

Khala shouted, "Arre! Children of God! Why don't you tell me the names of the Panchayat members? Let me also know."

Jumman said angrily, "Now, don't provoke me. It is your making, so you decide who you want to nominate."

Khalajaan understood the reason behind his anger and said, "Son, fear for God. A *Panch* is nobody's friend or foe. What a thing are you uttering! Okay! If you do not trust anybody here, you at least trust Alagu Choudhary. I shall nominate him as the *Sarpanch*."

Jumman Sheikh felt happy but hiding his feelings, he said, "okay! If Alagu, Alagu! For me Ramdhan or Alagu make no difference."

Alagu did not want to get himself entangled in this mess. He was biting his lips. He said, "*Khala,* you know very well that Jumman and I are very good friends."

Khala replied seriously, "nobody sells his honesty for the sake of friendship. God adorns the heart of a *Panch.* The words that the *Panchs* utter are actually the words coming straight from God. "

Alagu Choudhary became the *Sarpanch.* Ramdhan Mishra and the other enemies of Jumman cursed the old woman in their minds.

Alagu Choudhary said, "Sheikh Jumman, you and I are old friends. Whenever an occasion arose you have helped me and I too have been at your service whenever the need arose. But now, you and your old aunt are equal in my view. You may present whatever you want before the Panchayat."

Jumman was hundred percent sure that victory was his. Alagu was saying these things only for pretence. Therefore, he coolly replied, "*Panchs,* it's been three years since *Khalajaan* registered all her property in my name and I had agreed to provide her with food and clothing for life. God forbid I have not given her any trouble thus far. I consider her as my own mother. It is my duty to care for her. Of course between the women, there are small little differences. What control do I have over that? *Khalajaan* demands for money to meet her monthly expenses separately. The *Panchs* are not unaware of the value of the property. I do not get so much of income from it that I can give her monthly allowances separately. Moreover, the gift deed does not mention anything about monthly allowance. In that case, I would not have got into this entanglement even by mistake. That's all I want to say. The matter is now before the Panchayat. You may decide as you wish."

Alagu Choudhary used to work with the courts very often and hence he was a very law-abiding person. He started his cross-examination with Jumman. Every question of his was like the blow of a hammer. Ramdhan Mishra was very surprised with the questions. Jumman was shocked as to what was wrong with Alagu. Just a few minutes before Alagu was sitting beside him and talking so pleasantly with him. Within such a short time, he has turned the plate and is bent upon digging his roots. He did not understand which old feud he was avenging now. Is there no use of such a long friendship?

As Jumman Sheikh was musing over such thoughts, Alagu pronounced the judgement –

"Jumman Sheikh! The *Panchs* have discussed the case. They feel it is fair that *Khalajaan* gets a monthly allowance. It is our opinion that her property certainly fetches enough returns for you to give her a monthly allowance. This is our decision. If this is not acceptable to Jumman, the gift deed will stand cancelled."

As soon as Jumman heard this judgement, he became silent. 'My own friend treats me like an enemy and attacks me from behind, what can I call this but the changing times? The one whom I trusted most cheated me at the right time! These are occasions when the credibility of true friendship stands for a test. This is the friendship of *Kalyug* (the name of the present era). Why would the country not face the fury of such severe calamities when people are such cunning cheats? Diseases like plague and cholera are the punishments meted out for such misdeeds.'

But Ramdhan Mishra and the other Panchayat members were openly appreciating Alagu Choudhary for upholding the morality of the case. They said, "This is called Panchayat. It clearly differentiated the wrong from the right. Friendship is one thing but it is very important to support honesty. The planet runs only on the strength of such truthful persons else it may have doomed long ago."

This judgement shook the very roots of the friendship between Jumman and Alagu. Now they are not seen talking to each other. Such an old tree of friendship could not bear just one puff of truth. In reality it stood on a very weak soil of loose sand.

Now there was just a formal relationship between the two. They exchanged only basic courtesies. They used to meet but on a very sensitive footing like how a tender branch would meet a sharp sword.

His friend's deceit kept pricking Jumman all through the day. He kept thinking that he should somehow get an opportunity to avenge Alagu.

A lot of time is taken in the preparation of a good job but this is not so in the case of a bad job. Jumman too got the opportunity to take revenge very soon. Alagu bad bought a pair of fine oxen from Batesar just the previous year. They were of a foreign breed and had beautiful big horns. For months, people from all neighbouring villages came and looked at them with awe. Fortunately for Jumman, just one month after the Panchayat judgement against him, one of these oxen died. Jumman told his friends, "this is the punishment for cheating. Man may put up, but the God sees everything." Alagu started suspecting that Jumman would have poisoned his ox. His wife too blamed Jumman for this catastrophe, "Jumman has done something." One day there was a heated exchange of words between Alagu's wife and Kareeman over this matter. Both the women let a free flow of a river of vocabulary. The words were decorated with sarcasm, insult and metaphors.

Somehow Jumman brought things under control. He rebuked and advised his wife. He pulled her away from the battlefield. Choudhary used his intellectual and analytical approach to pacify his wife and make her understand.

What is the use of a single ox? He looked for a partner for this ox far and wide but could not find one. Finally there stood a suggestion that this ox should be sold off. There was one Samju Sahu in the village who rode a cart pulled by a single ox. He used to ferry loads of jaggery and ghee from the village to the market and bring back oil and salt from there to sell in the village. He was attracted by this ox. If he could get that ox, he undoubtedly could make three trips a day, while he could hardly make one trip a day at present. He went and examined the ox, took him on a test ride on his cart, bargained and fixed a price and brought the ox to his doorstep. He promised to pay the amount within a month. Choudhary too was concernedabout the sale and he did not pay much attention to the loss.

Samju Sahu felt he has to make the best use of the ox that he now possessed. He started making three to four trips a day. He never bothered to feed the ox with proper food or water. All that mattered to him was the number of trips he could make. He would take him to the market and spread some hay in front of him. The poor animal was not allowed to rest even for a while. He used to lead a relaxed life at Alagu Choudhary's house. Very rarely, he would be harnessed to a four-wheeled cart and it would happily run for miles together. The ox would be fed with fresh water, cooked lentils, husk with oil-cakes and sometimes even fresh ghee. Twice a day, an attendant would give him a wash, comb and caress him. Where was that luxurious life as compared to this drudgery all through the day! Within a month he shrunk. The moment he saw the yoke, he would turn bloodless. It was a great struggle to take every step. His bones were protruding. Though he was courageous, he could not bear the whippings that he got.

One day, Sahuji loaded the cart with double the weight during the fourth trip. The animal was tired of a full day's work and he could hardly lift his legs. But Sahuji kept lashing the poor animal with his whip. What else! The ox started moving with great difficulty. After running for a while, the ox felt like resting a while but Sahuji was in a great hurry to reach the destination and hence was heartlessly whipping the ox continuously. Once again the ox pulled up all his strength but failed miserably. He fell on the ground, never to get up. Sahuji beat him brutally, pulled his legs and poked his nostrils with his cane but would a dead animal ever arise? Only then Sahuji got suspicious. He looked at the ox intensely, unharnessed him and wondered how he could reach the cart home. He screamed and shouted but country roads close down by dusk just like the eyes of infants. Nobody was seen. There was no village nearby. He got furious and beat up the dead animal and cursed him, 'Wretched fool! If you had to die, couldn't you die after reaching home? Father-in-law dies midway! Who will draw the cart now?' Likewise, Sahuji kept cursing. He had sold a few bags of jaggery and few pots of ghee and hence had about two hundred and fifty rupees on him. The cart also had many bags of salt and thus he could not even leave the cart and go. Helplessly, he lay down in the cart. He decided to spend the night there. He smoked tobacco and *hookah* and sang. This way, he kept himself awake until midnight. He thought he was awake even thereafter but when day broke and his sleep vanished, he immediately felt his waist but the purse was gone. He got shocked and looked around and found even a few pots of oil missing. He was very upset and helplessly beat his head with his palms and swooned. He reached home early in the morning, moaning. When his wife heard about this unfortunate episode, she first cried and then started abusing Alagu Choudhary, "That wicked fellow has sold such a wretched animal that our life-time earnings are lost."

Many months passed by after this incident. When Alagu went to Sahu and demanded the price of his ox, Sahu and his wife started barking at him like provoked dogs – "Wah! Here we have lost our entire lifetime earnings and our life has been destroyed and you come here demanding for your dues! You gave us a dead ox and how dare you come here asking for its price! You took us for a ride and dumped your wretched ox on us! Do we look like helpless fools to you? We are also children of a *Baniya* (businessman). Go look for such fools elsewhere. First go wash your face in a ditch and then demand for money! If that is not agreeable to you, take our ox and go. Use him for two months if not for one. What else do you want?"

There was no dearth of people who wished bad for Choudhary. On such occasions, they too got together and strengthened Sahuji's claim. But it was not easy for Choudhary to wash his hands off a sum of one hundred and fifty rupees. He too got enraged at once. Sahuji angrily went inside to look for the lathi. Now his wife took charge. After a heated argument the feud seemed like turning into a fist fight. The woman went into the house and locked herself inside. Hearing the hulla-bulla many villagers gathered there. They tried to pacify both the parties. They gave assurance of safety to Sahuji and brought him out of his house. They told him that things cannot be decided in this fashion. They said, "let there be a Panchayat meet. Accept whatever is decided there." Sahuji agreed to this. Alagu too followed suit.

Preparations were made for the Panchayat meet. Both the parties were gathering supporters. On the third day, the Panchayat convened under the same tree. It was a similar evening. The crows were conducting their Panchayat meets in the fields. The issue there was whether they had rights over the peas-pods that were grown there and they decided to express their displeasure at the owner's calls to shoo them away until and unless the issue is settled! The flocks of crows sitting on the branches of the tree were questioning as to what right have these humans have to call them impolite when they do not hesitate to cheat their own friends!

The Panchayat started and Ramdhan Mishra said, "Why delay? We should elect the Panchayat members. Come on Choudhary! Whom do you nominate as the members?"

Alagu politely replied, "Let Samju Sahu himself nominate".

Samju stood up and said sternly, "From my side Jumman Sheikh."

The moment Alagu heard the name of Jumman Sheikh, his heart started pounding and he felt as though somebody had slapped him. Ramdhan was Alagu's friend. He intervened and asked "Alagu Choudhary, hope you have no objection".

Choudhary got disheartened and said, "No. Why would I object?"

Our sense of responsibility/answerability many times becomes reformer of our narrow-minded approach. When we forget the right path and get lost this sense becomes our trustworthy torch bearer.

An editor while sitting independently in his office, uses his popular writing skill to attack the legislature with full freedom and audacity. But there may come a time when he becomes a part of the legislature. The moment he dons the role of a politician, his style becomes insightful, rational and just. The reason behind this is the sense of responsibility. Youth are full of impudence. Parents worry a lot about them in that stage. They fear that they may bring ill-fame to their family. But once the burden of responsibility of the family falls on their shoulders the same disorganized, restless youth become so courageous and composed. This too is the result of the sense of responsibility.

In Jumman Sheikh's mind too, as soon as he donned the role of a *Sarpanch*, a sense of his responsibility arose. He thought he was now sitting on the highest pedestal of justice and truth. 'Whatever comes out of my mouth is in fact the diktat of the Almighty and my personal emotions should not influence my judgement. It is not right on my part to move even an inch away from truth.'

The *Panchs* started questioning both the parties. Both the parties kept justifying their deeds for a long time. Everybody was convinced that Samju Sahu had to definitely pay the cost of the ox. Just two of the members felt that Samju had to be given a discount because the he had lost a lot on account of the death of the ox. On the contrary, two other gentlemen felt that in addition to the original cost, Samju had to bear even a penalty as a punishment which will act as a deterrent to others from being so merciless in treating animals. In the end Jumman pronounced the judgement.

"Alagu Choudhary and Samju Sahu! The *Panchs* went into details of your case. It is only right that Samju pay up the original cost of the ox to Alagu. When he bought the ox, the ox was healthy. Had he paid up the cost at the time of sale, Samju could not have gone back on the deal today. The ox died because of the fact that it was made to slog beyond its capacity and was not also well taken care of. It was not fed properly."

Ramdhan Mishra said, “Samju consciously beat up the poor animal and hence he has to be meted out a punishment.”

Jumman said, “This is another issue. We are not concerned with that.”

Jagadu Sahu said, “Samju has to get some concession.”

Jumman said, “That depends on Alagu Choudhary’s discretion. If he wants to show some concession it will be out of his gracefulness.”

Alagu Choudhary could not control his happiness. He stood up and pronounced loudly, “Three cheers to *Panch Parameshwar* !

He was joined by many more from all sides, “Three cheers to *Panch Parameshwar!”*

Every person was praising Jumman’s morality. “This is called justice. This is not the job of a human being. God resides in *Panch Parameshwar*. This is His glory. Who can proclaim a lie as truth before Him?”

After a while, Jumman came to Alagu, embraced him and said, “*Bhaiyya,* from the moment you pronounced your judgement against me, I had become your worst enemy. But today I realized that sitting on the seat of a *Panch,* one can neither be a friend nor a foe to anybody. He thinks about nothing else except justice. Today I have got convinced that God speaks through the tongue of a *Panch.*” Alagu started weeping. The tears wiped away the scars in the minds of both of them. The creeper of friendship which had dried up once again sprang with life.

Boodhi Kaki - The Old Aunt

Most often childhood returns in our old-age. Kaki had tremendous craving for food and hence when she was not satiated enough, her discontentment took a very ugly form. She used to go to the extent of licking the leftover food from the plates of guests. The inhuman treatment meted out to aged persons will definitely bring tears in the eyes of the readers.

Most often childhood returns during old-age. Old Kaki had no other concern other than satiating her craving taste buds and she had no other weapon other than weeping to gain the attraction of others towards her want. She had lost all her other senses including her eye-sight and was totally crippled. She kept lying down all the time and cried incessantly if ever anybody spoke anything against her wish or her meal was delayed or her meal was insufficient or if some eatable arrived at home but was yet to be served to her. Her cries and sobs were not ordinary; she would scream out, tearing her throat.

It was long since her husband had passed away. Her children had also died in their youthful years. Now she had none but a nephew. She had written off all her wealth in the name of that nephew. The nephew had made tall promises while getting all her wealth transferred in his name but those promises remained like the superfluous promotional talk of the salesmen of low-grade shops. Though her assets yielded an annual income of not less than 150-200 rupees, the old woman got hardly fed proper food. It was not easy to say whether the fault lay with her nephew Pandit Buddhiram or his wife Srimathi Roopa. Buddhiram was a gentleman, as long as there was no harm done to his cash box. Roopa was caustic by behavior but God-fearing. Kaki was more disgusted by Buddhiram's nobility than by Roopa's rude behaviour.

Buddhiram sometimes felt sorry for his abusive attitude. He thought that he had earned a respectable status only because of the wealth that he got from Kaki. He had no problem if things could be improved by a few verbal assurances and dry sympathy but his good intentions got suppressed by his fear of the extra expenditure. He would get enraged if the old woman started lamenting inside the house, when some respectable guest waited at the door. He would go inside and scold her. Youngsters have a natural dislike for the elderly and when they saw such an attitude of their parents too, they troubled the old lady all the more. One of them would pinch her and run away, while another would spit gargled water at her. Kaki would scream aloud but it was widely understood that she always cried to eat and hence her moans and pains were ignored by all. Only when Kaki angrily abused the children, would Roopa arrive at the spot. Though Kaki used her verbal weapon sparingly in the fear of attracting Roopa, she felt that was more useful than her cries to free herself from distress.

In the entire family, if anybody had little sympathy for the old woman, it was Buddhiram's youngest daughter Laadli. She used to sit beside Kaki to munch her sweets to avoid her brothers snatching them from her. This was the most secure place for her, though she may have to share a little with the greedy Kaki. This was an easy way out to save herself from her unjust brothers. This selfish motive in both of them had brought a sort of sympathetic relationship between the two.

It was night time. The sound of *shehnai* was heard at the door of Buddhiram. The village children were enjoying the music with eager looks. Guests were resting on cots and getting themselves massaged by the barbers. A flatterer standing nearby kept reciting a list of titles in praise of Buddhiram and an engrossed audience kept acknowledging him with their 'Wah, wahs'. Buddhiram was so thrilled with these acknowledgements as he felt they were actually acknowledging him as a Chieftain. A few English-educated youth were disgusted over these happenings. They felt it was below their dignity to speak at or participate in such rural gatherings.

Today Buddhiram's eldest son Mukhram was getting engaged and the celebration was for that. The women were singing inside the house and Roopa was busy preparing food for the guests. Huge vessels were adorning the firewood stoves. On one stove *puris* and *kachories* were being fried while on another other items were being cooked. Spicy vegetables were being cooked in a huge vessel. The appetizing flavor of ghee and spices spread all over the place.

Old Kaki sitting in her room, seemed to be observing grief over her concerns. This delicious flavor made her restless. She was musing, 'possibly, I may not get any *puries* today. It is already so late and nobody brought my meals. All of them seem to have finished their lunch. Maybe nothing if left over for me.' This prompted her to cry but she could not cry since it was an auspicious day.

'Aah! What a delicious flavor! Who cares for me now! When getting even ordinary *roties* is a big challenge, am I fated to get a sumptuous meal of *puries*?' This thought saddened her and she had spasms of sorrow in her chest but fearing Roopa's outbursts, she kept silent.

Old Kaki was immersed in such sad thoughts for a long time. The aroma of ghee and spices broke the control over her mind. Her mouth started watering. Her heart was palpitating with the thought of tasty *puries.* 'Whom shall I call? Today Laadli too never turned up. Both the boys would always bother me but today, they too are not to be seen. I wish I had known what is happening.'

The images of *Puries* were dancing in her imagination. 'They might be well fried, tanned and puffed and yet soft. Roopa must have definitely eaten her lunch. The *kachories* must be smelling of *ajvain (*an aromatic seed) and cardamom. If I could just get hold of one *puri,* I would feel it. Why not I go and sit near the frying pan? *Puries* may be getting fried with an inviting 'hsss'. They may be getting removed from the pan and arranged on a huge plate. We can smell flowers at home too. But a garden is something different.' Thinking so, old kaki started creeping in the squatting position. She crept slowly and went and sat near the frying pan. On reaching there, she gained a sort of courage that hungry dogs have when they sit in front of people eating.

Roopa was perplexed with the preparations and moving around randomly. She kept going around from room to room and sometimes went near the stove, while sometimes into the store. Somebody came in from outside and said, "Maharaj is seeking for cool drinks" and Roopa gave him the drinks, while another person came in and said, "The flatterer has come. Give him something". Just as she was getting ready to pay something to the flatterer, the third person came in and said, "how long will it take for the lunch to get ready? Get the *dhol* and *majeera* (a kind of drum and cymbals) out." The helpless lonely woman was agitated of running around, getting worked up and irritated but found no opportunity to vent out her anger. She feared that the neighbourhood women might comment that she was getting provoked so easily. Her throat was dry out of thirst. She was perspiring because of the heat but found no time to drink a little water or fan herself for sometime. There was another fear that if at all she was not vigilant just for a moment, things could be plundered. In this state of mind, when she saw the old Kaki sitting beside the frying pan, she got enraged. She could not control her anger. She even forgot the presence of her friends from the neighbourhood there, who may think bad of her. What would the men-folk comment if they see her outburst. She pounced upon the old woman just as a frog would pounce on a worm, shook her with both her hands and said, "Such a fire in your stomach! Is it a stomach or a huge vessel? Had it become difficult for you to breathe inside your room? The guests have not yet eaten, why we have not even offered the food to the Gods. Don't you have patience to wait until such time? You have come and deposited yourself on our heads! May such a tongue get burnt! If you do not get to eat throughout the day, God knows in whose kitchen you will peep into! All the villagers will say, 'maybe the old woman does not get fed stomach full. That is why she roams around greedily!' The witch neither dies nor quits her bed. She is bent upon spoiling our name. She will die only after cutting our noses. She curses so much that we may turn into ashes! If you wish for good, go to your room. When everybody is served lunch, you too shall get your lunch. You are not some Goddess that you be worshipped first even before anybody else even drinks a drop of water!"

Old Kaki raised her head. She did not cry or utter anything. She crawled silently to her room. The voice was so bitter that it seemed that entire strength of the heart and brain, all the thoughts and the entire weight were directed towards the old woman. It seemed like water from all water bodies nearby rushing towards a river, whose bund has breached.

The lunch was ready. Plantain leaves were laid in the quadrangle and the guests had started eating. The women started singing tunes of festivity. The barbers and servants were also seated along with the guests but at a little distance. Etiquette demanded that nobody should rise until everybody finishes the meal. A couple of educated guests were getting restless that the servants were eating very slowly. They felt such a restriction was wasteful and useless.

The old Kaki was repenting in her room as to the state to which she had reached. She was not angry with Roopa. She felt sad at her own impatience. It is true that the hosts could not eat until and unless all the guests have been served lunch. She could not wait even until such time. She got insulted in front of everybody. She decided that until someone called her, she would not go.

She kept thinking on these lines and eagerly looked forward to someone coming to call her. But the aroma of the ghee was testing her patience. Each moment seemed like an age for her. 'Now the leaves would have been laid. The guests might have got ready. The barbers might be pouring water to the guests for washing their hands and feet. Looks like they have already sat to eat! Banquets songs are being sung'. Pacifying herself with such thoughts, she lay down on the cot. She started humming a tune. She realized that she had been singing for very long. 'what, will the guests be eating until now? I can hear nobody's voice. Definitely, the guests have eaten and left. Nobody came to call me. May be Roopa is angry and hence did not send for me. She must be thinking that I would go on my own and needed no invitation since I am not a guest.' The old woman got ready to move. The very hope that she would get to see tasty *puris* and spicy vegetables sent currents in her. She desired within her mind, 'first I will eat the *puris* with the vegetables, then with curds and sugar; *kachoris* would taste the best with *raytha*. Let anybody say anything, I will demand and eat to my fill. What else? People may think I am senseless. I don't care. I am getting to eat *puris* after such a long time. Can I just be satisfied with a lick or bite?'

Once again she squatted down and crawled towards the quadrangle. But unfortunately, as usual her desire had led her to estimate time wrongly. The guests were seated just then. A few of them were licking their fingers as they were having their lunch, while a few of them checking out whether they had finished their lunch. Some of them were gathering the *puries* served such that they did not slip outside the leaf, while some of them were enjoying curds. While yet a few others were asking for cups made of leaves, with hesitation, the old Kaki arrived amongst them. Many men were startled and stood up. They shouted, "Arre! Who is this old woman? How did she come here? Beware! Don't let her touch anybody."

Pandit Buddhiram raged with anger the moment he saw Kaki. He was holding a huge plate of *puries.* He banged the plate on the floor and just as a heartless money-lender would pull up a dishonest and cowardly debtor by his neck, as soon as he sees him, he held the old woman by both her hands and dragged her to the dark room and threw her forcefully. The hopeful garden was totally destroyed in just a moment of the hot summer winds.

The guests finished their lunch. Then the family members too had their lunch. The band members, dhobi and cobbler too finished their lunch but nobody bothered to enquire the old woman. Buddhiram and Roopa had both decided to punish the old Kaki for her shameless act. Nobody felt compassionate about her old-age, her helpless situation and senility. Only Laadli was feeling sad for her.

Laadli had a lot of love for Kaki. She was an innocent girl. There was no shade of naughtiness or restlessness in her like all other children. Both the times when she saw her parents dragging Kaki heartlessly, her heart wrenched. She wondered,'why are we not giving Kaki lots of *puries?* Will the guests eat away all the *puries?* What's wrong if Kaki ate before the guests ate? She wanted to go and pacify Kaki but fearing her mother, she could not go there. She had not eaten any of her share of *puries.* She had stored them in her toy box. She wanted to take those for Kaki. She was getting impatient. 'Old Kaki will sit up as soon as I tell her about this and feel very happy. She will love me a lot.'

It was eleven in the night. Roopa was sleeping in the quadrangle. Laadli could not sleep. The excitement of feeding Kaki with the *puries* kept her up. She had placed her toy box in the front. When she made sure that her mother was fast asleep, she got up silently and started thinking how she would go. Laadli spotted the neem tree in the front of her house. She realized that Lord Hanumanji was seated on the tree. She could clearly view his tail and mace (weapon usually carried by Hanuman, the monkey-God). She closed her eyes out of extreme fright. Just then the dog too sat up and Laadli felt emboldened. A running dog gave her more courage than many sleeping human beings. She lifted her box and set off towards the old Kaki's room.

The old woman could just remember that somebody dragged her by her hands and she felt like she was being flown over a hill. Her feet were banging against huge rocks and then somebody pushed her from the hill and she lost her consciousness.

When she woke up, she could not hear any sound. She thought that everybody had eaten their meals and slept, burying her fate along. 'How to spend the night? What should I eat? Her stomach was on fire with hunger. Ah! Nobody remembered me. Will they become richer by saving on my food? These people do not even have a bit of compassion for this dying old woman. Why should they displease her soul? Do I eat *roties* to fill my stomach or something else? Just for that, this state! I am blind and crippled. I can neither hear or understand anything. What if I went to the quadrangle, could Buddhiram not just say, 'Kaki, the guests are yet to eat. Come later.' He dragged me and pushed me. Roopa too rebuked me in front of everybody only on account of those *puries.* Even after I bore so much of insult because of those *puries*, their stone-hearts did not melt. They fed everybody and did not even bother about me. When they did not give me at that time, why would they give me now?' With these thoughts, she lay down happily discontented. She was chocking with sorrow but because of the fear of guests, she was not crying. Suddenly, she heard, "Kaki, wake up. I have brought *puries.*" Kaki recognized Laadli's voice. She sat up immediately. She groped for Laadli with both her hands and sat her up on her lap. Laadli took out the *puries* from the box and gave them to her.

Kaki asked, "Has your mother given these *puries*?"

Laadli replied, "No. These are my share."

Kaki gorged on the *puries.* In five minutes the box was empty. Laadli asked her, "Kaki are you full?"

Just as a scanty rainfall increases the heat in the atmosphere, these few *puries* aroused her hunger and desire all the more. She said, "No child. Go get some more from your mother."

Laadli said, "Amma is sleeping. If I wake her up, she will beat me."

Kaki shook the box once again. There were a few small scrapings in it. She kept wetting her lips and making sounds with her tongue.

Her heart was wringing as to how she could get more *puries.* When the dam of happiness breaches, the flow of desire becomes unlimited. Boozers become blind with intoxication with the very thought of intoxication. Kaki's impatient mind flowed in the strong flood of desires. The distinction between right and wrong kept vanishing. She controlled her desire for some time. Suddenly she told Laadli, "Please hold my hand and take me to the place where the guests had their meals."

Laadli could not understand her intention. She held Kaki's hand and took her to the place where all used leaves were dumped in the quadrangle. The poor senile and hungry old Kaki picked up the left-over pieces of *puries* from the leaves and gobbled them. 'Ah! How tasty was that curd! How soft, crisp and delicate were those *kachories*!' Though Kaki was senile, she did realize that she was doing something which she should not be doing. 'I am licking the used leaves of others.' But old-age is the last stage of thirst when all the desires get concentrated on one spot. In case of Kaki, that spot happened to be her taste buds.

Exactly at that time, Roopa woke up. She realized that Laadli was not beside her. She was startled and groped all the sides on the cot and also looked down, fearing that she might have fallen down. Not finding her nearby, Roopa got up and what did she see? Laadli was standing silently beside the dump of used leaves and Kaki was picking out pieces of left-over *puries* and eating them. Roopa was benumbed. She felt the shock and pain that she would feel when she sees someone slaughtering a cow. Nothing is sadder than a Brahmin driven to lick from others' used leaves. Just for a few pieces of *puries,* her unfortunate mother-in-law is indulging in such a pathetic act. This is a scene which sends shivers in the people who witness it. It seems like the earth stops rotating and the sky starts revolving. It seems a catastrophe is going to occur in this world. Roopa did not get angry. Whither anger in front of sorrow? She pointed her hand towards the sky and uttered genuinely, “Oh Almighty! Please show mercy on my children. Please do not punish me for this unfairness, lest I will be ruined!”

Roopa had never witnessed her selfishness and injustice in such real form. She pondered, ‘Oh! How heartless am I! This is the ill-fate of the one whose wealth has been fetching me an income of two hundred rupees! And that too because of me! Hey! Merciful God! I have committed a very great sin. Please pardon me. Today was my son’s betrothal ceremony. Hundreds of people have been served a feast. I remained a slave to their demands. To earn a good name, I spent hundreds of rupees, but I could not feed the one person, at whose grace I have consumed thousands of rupees, a full meal on this festive day! Only because of this reason, that old woman is helpless.’

Roopa switched on the light. She opened the doors of her store room. She filled a plate with all the varieties of food items and went towards Kaki.

It was past midnight and the plate of the sky was adorned with lakhs of stars. The Gods residing in them were decorating the sky with heavenly items but none of them would have enjoyed the extreme ecstasy that the old woman experienced on seeing a platter filled with so many goodies in front of her. Roopa said with a choked voice, “Kaki, get up and eat. I have committed a great sin today. Please do not mistake me. Please pray God to forgive me for my sins.”

Like innocent little children who forget all the rebukes and beatings that they received, on receiving some sweets, old Kaki was sitting and eating her meals, forgetting all that she had undergone that day. Every part of her only effused her sincere blessings and Roopa was witnessing that heavenly scene, experiencing its bliss.

Revenge

The excesses of exploitation result in revenge. Sometimes we also indulge in exploitation unconsciously but no sooner do we realize the truth, we repent. This is the complexity and also the speciality of human behavior.

Maya was standing on top of her three-storied house and was watching the road anxiously with worried eyes and wondering as to why he had not yet returned. 'Why this delay? He had written that he would be coming by this train only. The train must have arrived. Passengers are coming out of the station. There is no other train at this time. Maybe he is taking time unloading his baggages; maybe some of his friends went to greet him on his arrival and he will think of home only after they leave. He can after all tell his friends, 'please excuse me for now, we shall meet later.' But his soul lay in his friends.'

Tilothama – "He may be fetching me good toys."

Maya did not reply. Her expectation was turning into anger. She thought, 'I too will bother him just the way my Lord is bothering me. I will not talk to him for hours. He is sitting at the station even after arriving! He is enjoying hurting me. This has always been his way. But how shall I handle my heart? No, I really wish that I too will not enquire about him just the way he ignores me.'

Suddenly, a servant came up and said, "*Bahuji* (the way the daughter-in-law of the house is addressed by servants), there is a telegram from Lahore.

Maya was fuming within her. Her immediate thought was, 'what else would he have written except that he could not catch this train? Is it so difficult to send a telegram? Why don't I also send him a telegram stating that I will be gone to my mother's place for a month?' She told the servant, "go, leave the telegram on the table in the room." But on rethinking, she took the telegram and the moment she opened it, it fell off from her hand. It read,'Mr. Vyas was murdered by some criminal at ten tonight'.

Many months passed by. But the murderer could not yet be traced. The experienced detective police officers were working hard for finding clues. A twenty thousand reward was announced to anybody who could give a clue that leads to the arrest of the murderer. But there were no results.

Maya stayed in the same hotel where Vyas had stayed, for a month now. She had almost fallen in love with the room. Her face had changed beyond recognition in this time. But her face was not pale with pain or helplessness but was red with rage. Her intoxicating eyes were now blood-thirsty and blazen with vengeance. Every cell of her body was burning in the fire of vengeance. Now that was her life-time ambition and desire. The entire wealth of her love was now the driving force of her vengeance. She will cool down only when she witnesses the sufferings of that man, who had destroyed her life. The police detectives were trying to proceed based on the theory of fear and greed and search and investigation. But Maya adopted her own different way to reach her goal. Mr. Vyas was interested in ghost theories. She had some preliminary experience along with him. At that time, it was just an amusement for her. But now, that knowledge was her leverage. She kept improving her knowledge by trying out her skills on Thilothama. She was waiting for the day when she could invoke the soul of her husband and get some lead about the murderer from him. She was totally devoted in her job with great perseverance and concentration. It was ten in the night. Maya darkened the room and was practicing her skills on Thilothama. All of a sudden, she felt the presence of some holy personality in the room. She could see a flash of light which seemed like the brightness of a dying wick.

Maya enquired, "Who are you?"

Thilothama replied with a smile, "Don't you recognize me? I am your beloved, who was famous as Mr.Vyas in the world."

"You have come well in time. I want to know the name of your murderer".

"His name is Ishwar Das."

"Where does he live?"

"Shahjahanpur."

Maya enquired in detail about the house number, locality, facial features, etc. and noted them on a piece of paper. After some time, Thilothama sat up. When the room was lit up again, Maya's withered face was glowing with the happiness of victory. Her body was filled with waves of new vigor, like that of a traveler dying out of thirst finding water.

On the same night, Maya decided to proceed to Shahajanpur from Lahore.

It was night. The Punjab Mail was speeding as if tearing the darkness. Maya was in a second class compartment, thinking about various things like the place where she would stay in Shahjahanpur, her plan to search for the murderer's house and ways to avenge him. Thilothama was sleeping ignorant of everything beside Maya and the man on the front berth was sleeping like a log.

Suddenly the door of the compartment opened and two men in suits entered the compartment. They both were Englishmen. They sat on either side of Maya. Maya shrunk herself and felt bad that they sat in such a way. She felt like asking them to sit on the other side, but the woman who had set out to avenge her husband's murder was shivering of that immediate danger that she was in. The two devils went closer to her, seeing her shrinking herself. Maya could no longer sit there. She got up and was about to go to another berth, when one of them caught her hand. Maya struggled to release herself and said, "Hope your doomsday has not arrived. Let go my hand you pig."

At this, the second man got up and hugged her tight. He spoke in faltering voice, "Well! We will give you a lot of money."

Maya tried to push him away with all her strength and said, "Move out you scoundrels or else I will break your heads."

The second man too got up and both of them were trying to lay her down on the berth. Suddenly, the man on the upper berth woke up hearing the noise. He saw the indecent act of the scoundrels and jumped down. The two men let Maya go and started kicking that man. Both of them were raining blows on him, while he was trying to save himself with his hands. He got no chance of retaliating. Then suddenly, he leapt up and removed a knife from under his bedding. He gathered himself, pointed it at the men and said, "if you both do not get out of this compartment right now, I will kill both of you."

The two men did get shocked seeing the knife, but they too were not unarmed. One of them removed a revolver and pointing it towards that man, said, "Get out rascal."

Maya was shivering at the impending danger. Danger brings out all our hidden courage. When we are in danger, we trespass the boundaries of fear and do things at which we ourselves wonder. The same Maya, who was shivering out of fear, pounced at the white man like a cat, snatched the revolver from him and threw it out of the train. The man tried to bite her with anger but she quickly withdrew her hand and pulled the train's emergency chain. The other man, who had no weapon on him, was standing at the edge, fearing the knife. When he saw Maya pulling the chain, he opened the door and started running. His companion too started following him. Just then, the man with the knife pushed him hard and he fell with his face down. Then he started punching, kicking and slapping him so much that his mouth started bleeding. By then the train stopped and the guard was walking towards the compartment with his lantern.

But the two demons jumped out of the train, without second thoughts and vanished into the darkness. The guard also did not attempt much to catch them, as it would be very difficult to locate them in that darkness. There were deep valleys on either side, where let alone two, even two hundred men could easily hide themselves. The train left after ten minutes.

Maya took a sigh of relief and said, "I dread what would have been my fate, had you not been here today! God only knows! Hope you have not been hurt".

That man put back the knife into his pocket and said, "Never. I was so fast asleep that I did not know when those two idiots came into the compartment. Otherwise, I would not have allowed them to step in. I will lodge a complaint at the next station."

Maya: "No! That will only put us to shame and tension. There is no use reporting. God has taken care of me today. Even now my heart is beating so loudly. Where are you travelling up to?"

"I need to go to Shahjanpur."

"I too need to go there. What is your name? Let me at least know the name of my protector".

"I am known as Ishwar Das."

Maya's heartbeat stopped for a second! This must be that murderer. His features match with those that were explained to her. She enquired with fear, "Which locality do you live in?"

"I live in ...."

Maya felt shocked. She looked out of the window and took a deep breath. Oh! Even though the murderer has been found, the situation is such that she is now drowned in his obligation! Could she make this man the target of her dagger, when being a total stranger, merely out of compassion, he had helped her at a moment of crisis? He had risked his life! She was in a strange fix. She looked at his face and she could find only decency there. She doubted how such a man could commit a murder.

Ishwar Das enquired, "Aren't you coming from Lahore? Where do you want to go in Shahjanpur?"

"Right now, I will stay in some *Dharamshala* (a lodging facility at charitable rates). I have to find a house."

Ishwar Das enquired with a surprise, "Then, you are not visiting any relative or friend in Shahjahanpur?"

"I will find somebody or the other."

"Where is your original home?"

"I originally hail from Lucknow. Now, I have no home. I am a widow."

Ishwar Das fixed up a good house for Maya at Shahjahanpur. He also arranged for a servant. He visited her on some days to check on her welfare. However much she tried to avoid getting obligated to him or building intimacy with him, she was compelled to do so because of his honesty, decency and polite behaviour.

One day he brought some pots and furniture items. He had brought some beautiful wall hangings too. Maya irritatingly said, “I have no interest in these ornamental pieces. You are taking unnecessary trouble.”

Ishwar Das felt shy as though he had committed a mistake, and justified his action saying, “These things were lying uselessly in my house. So, I brought them here.”

“I do not want to become a slave to these items of empty vanity.”

Ishwar Das hesitatingly replied, “if you are so uncomfortable, shall I take them back?”

Maya saw his eyes welling up with tears and said out of compulsion, “Now that you have already brought them, let them be. But please do not get such things in future.”

One day Maya’s servant did not turn up. She waited for him until nine O’Clock and then started washing the used vessels. She had never done this job in her life. She pitied herself for her present condition and felt like crying. There was a time when there was a platoon of servants in her house and here now she is forced to wash the vessels on her own! Thilothama was running around doing small little errands with full vigour. She was not bothered. There was no limit to her joy in getting this opportunity to work and prove her usefulness and importance. Just then Ishwar Das came in and seeing Maya washing the vessels, he said, “what are you doing? Just let them be! I will arrange for a man right now. Why did you not inform me? Hey Ram! Come out!”

Maya carelessly replied, “No problem. Don’t take any trouble. I will wash the vessels myself.”

“What’s the need? I will be back in a minute.”

“No. Please don’t get anybody. I can wash these many vessels easily.”

“Okay. Then, let me also give you a hand.”

Saying this, he ran out with a bucket to fetch water. He brought the water and started washing the vessels which she had brushed with soap.

Maya tried snatching the vessel from his hand and said, "why are you embarrassing me? Let it be. I shall wash them myself."

"Am I embarrassing you or you are embarrassing me? You are a visitor here and I am a native of this place and it is my duty to serve you. You made the first mistake by not informing me and now this is your second mistake. I cannot bear this."

Ishwar Das washed all the vessels in no time. Looked like he was used to doing such errands! He washed all the vessels and filled them with water. Wiping off the sweat from his forehead, he said, "Tell me if you want anything from the market. I shall fetch them right now."

Maya: "No please! Excuse me and go home.

Ishwar Das: "Thilothama! Come on! I shall take you around the town today."

Maya: "No please! Just let it be. She will not go out now."

Maya uttered these words with such sternness that Ishwar Das was disparaged. He did not say anything again. He left silently. After he left, Maya felt she had been too rude towards him. After that incident in the train, there was ever a clash going in her mind between vengeance and humaneness. She shuddered thinking what could have happened to her on that day, had he not arrived as a God-sent messenger and a sense of gratitude would swell up from the depth of her heart towards Ishwar Das. Could she stain her hands with the blood of a person to whom she has such a great obligation? But only because of him, she was pushed to such an unfortunate situation. Only because of him had she undertaken that journey by train all alone. Otherwise, why would she travel without any friend or help? Only because of him she is undergoing the pains of widowhood and she would have to experience it all her life. Her eyes reddened on these thoughts and she let out a hot breath. She felt like taking a dagger at once and finishing him.

Today, Maya made her final decision. She had invited Ishwar Das home for a feast. This will be his last feast. Of course he had definitely done a favour to her. But will a favour or a good deed put out the fire of her grief? Ishwar Das came home at nine in the night. Maya filled her voice with cordiality and said, "Please have your seat. Shall I fetch hot *puries*for you?"

Ishwar Das: "Are you still waiting for me? You have taken unnecessary trouble in this hot weather."

Maya placed a plate before him and said, "I do not know how to cook. If you do not like any item, please excuse me."

Ishwar Das relished each and every item served and appreciated her profusely. He had never eaten such tasty dishes in his lifetime.

"You were saying you never knew how to cook."

"So what, did I say anything wrong?"

"Definitely wrong! You have proved your own mistake. I had never tasted such delicacies in my life."

"You are flattering me. That's okay. Go on."

"No, I am not flattering. I am speaking the truth. Which of these items shall I not appreciate? I wish I could find some shortcoming, but I cannot think of one. If I invite my friends for a feast, I will trouble you."

"Please do trouble me! I am ready."

It was ten by the time he finished dinner. Thilothama had slept. The street went silent. As Ishwar Das got ready to leave, Maya said, "Would you want to go away? Why can't you sleep over here? I somewhat feel frightened. You can sleep in the room outside and I shall sleep in this quadrangle."

Ishwar Das thought for a minute and said, "Okay! Fine! You had never expressed before that you were scared to sleep in this house. I would have arranged for an elderly woman to sleep with you."

Ishwar Das settled down in the room and Maya went inside to have her dinner. But not a morsel went down her throat! Her heart beat loudly and some sort of fear loomed over her. Suppose Ishwar Das wakes up all of a sudden? How shameful would it be on her!

Maya had sharpened the dagger well. She had practiced handling it all through the day. She would attack with such force that it would not go waste. Even if Ishwar Das wakes up, he will be fatally wounded.

It was midnight and Ishwar Das's loud snores fell on her ears, Maya got up with her dagger but her entire body was shivering. Fear and determination, attraction and hatred simultaneously lead her forward one moment but pull her back the other. She felt that the entire house and the sky were revolving fast; every item in the room seemed to be going round. But in a moment, this restlessness gave way to immense fear. She tip-toed to Ishwar's room but her feet got fixed over there. Tears started flowing out of her eyes. 'Oh! How weak am I? I am not able to avenge the man who has destroyed my life, who has shattered my green fields, barrened my lovely blooming garden and dumped me into a burning pyre forever! After all, they were my own sisters who took up swords and guns in their hands and fought in the battlefields; sat on the burning pyres with smiles on their faces!' At that time, she felt that Mr.Vyas was standing before her and motivating her to move forward. He seemed to be saying, 'Won't you avenge my murder? My soul is longing for revenge. Will you let it suffer so forever? Is this the vow of loyalty?' These thoughts swayed Maya's feelings. Her eyes turned blood-red. She bit her lips with her teeth and tightened her fist on the handle of the dagger. She was filled with a sort of obsession. She just stepped into the room, while Ishwar Das opened his eyes. The room was dim-lit with a lantern. He was shocked when he heard Maya's footsteps and froze at what he saw – Maya appeared like calamity personified and she was approaching him with a naked dagger in her hand.

He got up from the cot and said with fear, "what happened sister? Why are you holding this dagger?"

Maya said, "This dagger is thirsty for your blood because you have murdered my husband."

Iswar Das paled. He said, "Did I?"

"Yes! You did! You were the one who murdered my husband in Lahore, where he had gone to conduct a case. Can you deny this? My husband's soul has directly informed your address to me."

"So, you are Mr.Vyas' wife."

"Yes. I am his unfortunate wife and you are the one who has widowed me. It is true that you have favoured me but those favours cannot extinguish the fire in my heart. It can be cooled only with your blood."

Ishwar Das looked at Maya pleadingly and said, "If this is your final decision, go ahead. I am ready. If my blood can put out the fire in your heart, I will shed my blood voluntarily at your feet. But just as you feel it is your duty to quench the thirst of your sword with my blood, I too felt dutybound to murder Mr.Vyas. You know he had gone to Lahore to conduct a political law suit. But I could not bear the manner in which he used his exemplary knowledge of law in assisting the police in fabricating false evidences and heartlessly and mercilessly destroyed the lives of many young, helpless men, who were innocent. Those days, there would be a huge crowd of onlookers in the court premises and they all would leave, blaming Mr.Vyas. But I knew the actual facts of the case. Thus my conscience could not be satisfied just by blaming or scolding Mr.Vyas. What can I tell you? Mr. Vyas very consciously and deliberately proved falsehood as truth. He was the cause for bringing darkness to so many houses. Today so many mothers are shedding tears of blood with the pain of losing their sons and so many women are burning in the fire of widowhood! We don't care the excesses committed by the police, as we do not expect anything better from them. The police force is filled with greedy, illiterate and cruel rogues. The Government has systematized this on a permanent basis only to give trouble to its subjects. But we hope to get justice from advocates. We respect them. They belong to the highest cadre of most vigilant and educated populace. When we find such people becoming the puppets in the hands of the police, our anger crosses limits. I was an admirer of Mr.Vyas. But when I witnessed him coercing innocent under-trials to make false confessions, I started hating him. Poor under-trials were being hanged by legs for days together, just to confess to crimes which they never committed. Red chillie powder used to be thrust into their noses. Mr. Vyas was not just a witness to such excesses but rather he himself was directing the police to indulge in such acts.

The stiffness on Maya's face started easing. Instead, genuine anger started glowing. She asked, "Do you have any evidence in support of your claim that he indulged in such tortures?"

"All these facts were very commonly known. Every child of Lahore knew about this. I have been an eye witness. What other evidence can I produce? The only fault of those helpless beings was that they were the true friends of Hindustan and spent all their time in educating and serving her citizens. They would fast to hold the police from torturing innocent public and that was their crime. Mr.Vyas was the right hand of the police in punishing these people for the crime."

The dagger fell off Maya's hands. Her eyes welled-up with tears and she said, "I never knew that he could do such things."

Ishwar Das said, "Don't think that I am accusing Mr.Vyas falsely fearing your sword. I never cared for my life any time. Who is waiting to cry over my death that I should care for my life? If you feel I have committed an improper murder, then lift the dagger and put an end to my life. I will never obstruct you. If you are unable to do that, call the police, who will very easily lift me off this earth. It is not difficult to get proof. I could confess on my own to the police, but I do not consider this as a crime. If hundreds of lives can be saved with the death of one person, then that is not murder. I wish to live only because I may be required once again under similar circumstances."

Maya said weeping, "If at all your statements are true, I pardon you. God will decide whether you did right or wrong. I request you to give me the addresses of the homes that were shattered by my husband so that I could be of some service to those families."

The Chess Players

When a game becomes a vice, then honour, prestige, duty – everything takes a back-seat. Even when the city is attacked, the king continues playing chess in the ruins. But when the issue of self-respect and dignity is raised, he shoots sharp verbal arrows and even raises his swords. The soldier of chess bleeds not on the battlefield but in the field of his honour!

It was the rule of Wajid Ali Shah. Lucknow was immersed in the colours of entertainment. Small, big, rich and poor were all fully drowned in amorous acts. While some spent their time in music and dance, others enjoyed smoking *afim(*a kind of intoxicating drug). Merriment gained prominence in every factor of life – governance, literature, social system, art and crafts, industry and trade, food and commerce –coquetry ruling all over. The employees of the state were busy indulging themselves in worldly pleasures, the poets in describing love and separation, the crafsmen were busy creating artworks with silk thread and *chikkan* embroidery, businessmen in trading in various products of beauty like collyrium, perfumes, body lotions and pastes. But everybody's eyes were intoxicated with coquetry.Nobody had an inkling of the happenings of the world. Peacocks were fighting. Partridges were being bred only to be killed. Dice game boards were spread in places and shouts of victory filled the air. Severe battles of chess were fought in places. Everybody right from the emperor to the commoner was submerged only in this din. Things had reached such a state that if beggars were offered alms, instead of feeding themselves, they ended up consuming liquor or *afim.* The brains get sharpened by playing chess and card games. Analytical acumen gets enhanced; it becomes a habit to find solutions to complicated issues. Such rationalisations were vehemently put forth all over (there is no dearth of such people even today). Therefore what was the problem for any intellectual if Mirza Sajjad Ali and Mir Roshan Ali spent most of their time sharpening their intellect? Both of them had unlimited *jagirs* (land) and they had no problems of livelihood and hence sat at home and indulged in gambling. After all what else did they have to do? Early in the morning, the two friends would have their breakfast and set the chess board ready. Then the fight of the pawns would begin. Then they would never realize when the clock crossed noon, when the day dimmed into evening and when sun started setting. Repeated calls from inside the house were made once in a while that the meals were ready. "Okay. We'll be there shortly. Set the table."The cook would get tired of calling them and supply the meals to the friends at the same place that they were playing and they would continue the game, while eating in between moves. There were no old people and hence the contests were held right in his *Deewankhane* (Hall of Audience). But nobody cared about whether the other people living with him were happy with this practice. Let alone the family members, even the neighbours and the servants working for him made hateful criticisms about this, "Very depressing game! It destroys the household. God forbid, nobody should get addicted to this game. The person becomes useless both for the family and the society. A very bad disease indeed!" Things had gone so worse and Mirza's wife hated this practice so much that she would find some reason or the other to pick on her husband. But she got such opportunities very rarely, because she would still be asleep when the game board would already be spread and the Mirza would get back only late in the night after she slept. True! She would vent out her anger on the servants: "What, he has ordered for drink? Let him come and take it.They do not have time to eat their meals? Go and throw the food on their heads! Let them eat or feed the dogs!" But she could not say anything in person, because she did not have as much anger against her husband, Mirza Saheb, as she had against Mir Saheb. He had fully spoilt the title Mir that adorned his name! Maybe Mirzaji passed on all the blame on Mir Saheb to defend himself.

One day, the Begum (Mirza's wife) had a severe headache. She told the girl, "Go fetch Mirza Saheb. Let him get some medicine from some *Hakim* (native doctor). Come on, quick!" When the girl went to the Mirza, he said, "Go. I'll come in a minute." The Begum's temper was hot. How can she bear with the fact that the Mirza would play chess, while she suffered a headache? Her face drained. She told the girl, "Go and tell him, 'come immediately. Otherwise, she will go to the *Hakim* on her own.'" Mirzaji was at a very interesting stage in the game, when just in two moves, he would be defeating Mir Saheb. He said with irritation, "What is it so life-threatening? Can she not have some patience?"

Mir: "Arre! Why don't you go and talk to her? Women are of weak tempers."

Mirza: "Oh yes! Why wouldn't you want me to go? After all, you are going to get defeated in two more moves!"

Mir: "*Janaab*, don't get taken away by such a belief! I have thought of such a move that your pawns will remain safe but still you will get defeated! Go listen to her. Why do you want to unnecessarily hurt her?"

Mirza: "Now, I will definitely defeat you and then only go."

Mir: "I will not make my move. You go talk to her and return."

Mirza: "Arre *yaar*! I have to go to the *Hakim!*The headache is not genuine. It is just an excuse to bother me."

Mir: "Whatever it is, for her sake, you have to do this."

Mirza: "Okay! I shall make just one more move."

Mir: "Surely not! Until and unless you go and talk to her, I will not touch the pawns."

Mirza Saheb was compelled to go inside. The Begum changed her tone but said in a shaky voice, "You are so obsessed with this chess. You will not get up even if somebody is dying. God forbid, some man becomes like you!"

Mirza: "What shall I say? Mir Saheb never agrees to stop the game. After a lot of difficulty I have been able to free myself from his pestering."

Begum: "What, does he think everybody else is as useless as he himself is? He too has a family of wife and children or has he cleared them away?"

Mirza: "Very adamant man! Whenever he comes, I am forced to play."

Begum: "Why don't you reprimand him?"

Mirza: "He is of similar age and is two inches taller than me. I have to put up with him."

Begum: "Then I will reprimand him myself. He might get upset; let him get. Who is after the other's bread? If the Queen gets angry, she will be the loser; she will be widowed. Hariya, go out and get the chess board. Inform Mir Saheb that the Mirza will not continue the game and hence he can go home."

Mirza: "Hold on! Don't ever do such things! Do you want to defame me? Wait Hariya, where are you off to?"

Begum: "Why don't you let her go? He is after my blood and you want to encourage him. Okay. You stopped Hariya. Will you be able to stop me?"

Saying this, Begum Saheba angrily walked towards the Diwankhaana. Poor Mirza went pale. He begged his wife, "I promise on Hazrath Hussain! Please understand my position. Don't go there". But the Begum did not listen to him. She reached the door of the Diwankhaana but she suddenly stopped there, dreading to go and face an outside male folk. She peeped in and coincidentally the room was empty. Mir Saheb had rearranged a couple of pawns and strolling outside, while planning how to defend himself. Begum entered the room, pulled out the chess board, threw a few pawns below the bed and a few outside. Then she closed the door and latched it from inside. Mir Saheb, who was outside saw the pawns flying out of the window and heard the jingling sound of bangles. When he heard the door being shut, he understood that the Begum was really very upset. He silently went home.

Mirza said, "you have done something very strange."

Begum: "If Mir Saheb ever comes here, I will stand here and see him off. If one had this much of obsession for God, one could have earned deliverance! You keep playing chess and I have to break my head about managing the kitchen. Will you now go to the *Hakim* or you still have some objection?"

Mirza left home but instead of going to the *Hakim,* he went to Mir Saheb's house and elaborated everything that happened. Mir Saheb said, "the moment I saw the pawns flying out of the window, I grasped everything. I ran out immediately. She seems to be a very short-tempered woman. But I cannot believe that you have given her so much of liberty. How is she concerned about what you do outside the house? It is her duty to maintain the household and why should she bother about other things?"

Mirza: "Okay! Now, please tell me, when and where shall we play?"

Mir: "Why worry so much? After all, my house is so big. Let's play here."

Mirza: "But how can I pacify Begum Sahiba? I was all the time at home and yet she was so upset. Now, if I come here, she may not spare me alive!"

Mir: "*Aji!* Let her bark! She will come around in three or four days. All you have to do from today is to become a bit haughtier."

Mir Saheb's wife, for whatever obvious reasons, preferred Mir Saheb to stay away from home. Therefore, she never commented anything about his obsession for chess and in fact she herself reminded him of his game, when he sometimes got delayed. So, Mir Saheb thought that his wife was very well-behaved and decent. But when the game started being organized in her own house and Mir Saheb started staying home most of the time, she found it very difficult. Her health started deteriorating. She yearned to peep out of the door all day.

The servants started gossiping. Till then, they were whiling away their time all day long. They were not concerned as to who came home or who went out. But now, theirs became an eight-hour duty. Sometimes, they were asked to fetch *paan,* while sometimes sweets. Hukkah was on all the time like the burning heart of a beloved. They kept complaining to the Begum, "*Miya's* chess has become a pain in our neck. Our feet are full of blisters running around all day. What sort of obsession is this that they sit early in the morning and it goes on till night. It is fine to play for an hour or half just to entertain oneself. Anyway, we have no complaints. After all we are

Huzoor's slaves; it is our duty to heed to his orders. But this game is very inauspicious. One who plays this never flourishes. Some ill fate will strike the household definitely. We have seen great households of an entire locality getting destroyed one after another! The entire locality is discussing about this. We are obliged to *Huzoor* and how can we bear to hear ill of him? But what can we do?" The Begum said, "I personally do not like this game. But he never listens to anybody. What can be done about this?"

The few old-timers who lived in the locality started cooking up varieties of imaginary stories of inauspicious events, "This is no good. When this is the state of the rich, the kingdom has to be saved only by God. The Kingdom will get destroyed with this royal game. This is a sign of ill-fate."

There was chaos in the entire kingdom. The public were looted in broad daylight. There was nobody to listen to their woes. The wealth from the rural places was brought to Lucknow and spent on prostitutes, liquor and other kinds of vices. The credit of English companies kept rising. The lotus flowers were getting heavier with wetness! As there was anarchy, even the annual taxes were not being collected properly. The Resident (officer) kept giving warning signals time and again but all those went unheard by the people, who were totally intoxicated in pleasure games.

Well! Months passed by since the game being set at the Diwaankhaana of Mir Saheb. Newer plans were being thought of; newer fortresses were being put up; every day newer battle strategies were being planned. Sometimes, quarrels resulted during the game and went to the extent of a break-up but very soon the friends got back together. Sometimes, the game would be stalled and Mirza Saheb would go home angrily. Mir Saheb would go into his house. But a whole night's sleep would bring peace and endall differences. Early in the morning the two friends would arrive at the Diwaankhaana.

One day the two friends were sitting and deceiving each other in the swamp of chess. Just then an officer of the emperor's army arrived on his horse looking for Mir Saheb. Mir Saheb was taken aback. Now, what is this new headache? Why this enquiry? This does not seem to be a good omen! He shut the doors of the house and told his servants to inform the officer that he was not at home.

Officer: “Not at home? Where is he then?”

Servant: “I do not know. What’s the matter?”

Officer: “How can I tell you what the matter is? The summons is for the Saheb. Maybe there is a request for some soldiers for the army. Is he a *jagirdar* or *a joker?* Onewill realize the value of groceries only when he goes to the battlefield.”

Servant: “Okay fine. You can go. I will inform him.”

Officer: “There is nothing to inform him. Tomorrow I myself will come. I have orders to take him along.”

The Officer left. Mir Saheb was shivering. He told Mirza, “*Janab*, what will happen now?”

Mirza: “We are in deep trouble. Hope I am also not beckoned.”

Mir: “The wretched fellow has said he would come again tomorrow.”

Mirza: “Disastrous! What else? If we have to go to the battlefield, we have to meet an untimely death.”

Mir: “There is only one way to escape. We should never be available at home. From tomorrow, let us set the game at some God-forsaken spot on the bank of river Gomathi. Who will know about us? Let the officer come and go back empty-handed.”

Mirza: “Oh God! Such a brilliant idea! There is no other way out.”

Mir Saheb’s wife told the Officer, “You gave them a good message.”

The Officer replied, “I can make such stupid men dance to my tunes at the snap of my fingers. They have lost their entire valour and intellect to chess. Now, they will never be at home even by mistake.”

From the next day onwards, the two friends set out of their homes in the darkness of early hours. They squeezed a small carpet under their arms, packed some eatables in a box and went towards a deserted old Masjid built by Nawab Asafaudulla on the other bank of river Gomathi. On their way, they picked up some tobacco, hukkah pot and liquor. They would spread the carpet at the Masjid, fill the hukkah pot with tobacco and start playing chess. Then they would forget the whole world. Other than a couple of words such as 'check' or 'checkmate' nothing else would be uttered by the two of them. Perhaps even a Yogi would not be so concentrated in his state of *Samadhi (*trance). In the afternoon, when pangs of hunger struck them, they would go to some small eatery and have their lunch. Then they would again fill the hukkah and get engrossed in their battlefield of chess. On some occasions, they would even forget to have their lunch.

The political situation of the state was getting worse. The East India Company's army was advancing towards Lucknow. There was chaos in the city. People were fleeing from the city to the countryside, along with their children. But our two players had the least concern about all this. They took to narrow streets when they went out of their homes, in the fear that they would not be spotted by any messenger of the emperor and caught unnecessarily. They wanted to squander *jagirs* worth thousands of rupees doing nothing.

One day, the two friends were playing chess at the ruins of the Masjid. Mirza's game was a bit weak. Mir Saheb was calling check after check against Mirza. Just then, they saw a few soldiers of the English approaching them. It was the army of the whites, that was coming to sieze Lucknow.

Mir Saheb said, "The English army is approaching. God save us."

Mirza: "Let them come. Save yourself. Make the next move."

Mir Saheb: "We have to check out. Let's hide behind these bushes."

Mirza: "we will take a watch later; What's the hurry? Take care of this check."

Mir: "There is a tank also. There may be around 5000 soldiers. Such smart youth! Faces red like those of monkeys! Their very faces look terrorizing."

Mirza: "*Janab*, do not try diverting my attention. You try this strategy with somebody else. Now, check."

Mir: "You are a very strange person. A catastrophe has struck our city but you are bothered about your wager! Do you have any idea as to how we can reach home, if the city falls into the hands of the English?"

Mirza: "When the time to leave comes, we shall see. Now the move! The game lies in just this move."

The army moved away. It was ten in the night. Once again the board was set.

Mirza: "What about our dinner today?"

Mir: "*Aji*, today is *roza* (fast of the month of Ramzaan). Are you feeling hungrier?"

Mirza: "No, no. I don't know what is happening in the city."

Mir: "Nothing would have happened there. People would be sleeping after their dinner. His Highness Nawab Saheb will also be enjoying in his palace."

It was three in the morning, when the two gentlemen sat for their next game. Now, Mirza's game was weak. At around four, they could hear the sounds of the retreating army. The captured Nawab Wajid Ali was being taken to an unkown place by the army. There was no chaos or unrest in the city. Not a drop of blood was shed. Till that day, there could not have been such a peaceful defeat of an independent state, without bloodshed. This was not the kind of non-violence with which the Gods would be pleased. This was indeed such cowardice that even the worst cowards would cry over! The Nawab of the vast Awadh kingdom was going as a prisoner while the city of Lucknow was fully asleep intoxicated in its luxuries. This was the ultimate step of the political downfall.

Mirza Saheb said, "*Huzoor*, the tyrants have arrested Nawab Saheb".

Mir: "May be! Come on, take this check on your King."

Mirza: "*Janab*, please hold on. My mind is not here at this moment. The poor Nawab might be shedding tears of blood at this time."

Mir: "Of course, he has to weep! Will he get all these pleasures there? Here is my check."

Mirza: "All days are not the same. Such a painful situation!"

Mir: "That's true. Take this! Another check! This is decisive. You cannot escape."

Mirza: "Oh God! You are really heartless! You are not moved even by such a big catastrophe. Oh! The poor Wajeed Ali Shah!"

Mir: "First save your King; you can then mourn for Nawab Saheb! This check and your defeat! Give me your hand!"

The army left with the emperor. Immediately after they passed by, Mirza set the game once again. The wound of defeat is very painful. Mir said, "Come on, let us sing an elegy to mourn Nawab Saheb's defeat." But Mirza's patriotism was lost in his personal defeat. He was intent upon avenging his defeat.

It was evening. Bats started barking in the ruins. The swallows held on to their nests. But the two players were totally concentrated such as two blood-thirsty warriors fighting with each other. Mirzaji had lost three games in a row; the state of the fourth game too was not very positive. Every time, he decided to win the game and played very carefully; but some move or the other spoilt his bet. His vengeance was getting stronger with every defeat. Mir Saheb on the other hand was singing *gazals* joyfully and snapping his fingers as if he had discovered a hidden treasure. Mirzaji was getting irritated with this and was trying to hide the insult of his defeats by justifying his moves. But as the wager was getting weaker, he was losing his confidence. So much so, he started getting irritated for every thing and said, "*Janab*, you please do not change your move. You made a move and then took that back. Whatever move you decide, you make it in one go; why are you holding on to the pawn? Leave it alone. Until you decide your move, dare not touch the pawn! You take almost half-an-hour for every move. This is not allowed. If one takes more than five minutes for a move, it should be considered as his defeat. Again you shifted your pawn! Keep it back silently."

Mir Saheb's soldier was about to fall. He said, "When did I make a move?"

Mirza: "You have already made the move. Keep the pawn back in the same square."

Mir: "Why should I keep it there? When did I release the pawn out of my hand?"

Mirza: "If you hold on to the pawn till the doomsday, do you mean to say there will be no move? Knowing that your soldier was about to fall, you have started creating trouble."

Mir: "You are creating trouble. Victory or defeat is fated. Nobody can win by cheating."

Mirza: "So, you have lost this game."

Mir: "How do I lose this game?"

Mirza: "Then place the pawn back in that square, where you had placed it before."

Mir: "Why should I put it there? I will not do that."

Mirza: "Why not? You have to."

The quarrel intensified. Both of them held on to their stand. Neither of them gave up. Irrelevant issues arose. Mirza said, "One would know the rules of the game, only if anybody from the family had ever played chess! They were merely mowing grass and how can you play chess?Royal status is something that should have handed down by ancestors. Merely by getting a few *jagirs*, one doesn't become royal."

Mir: "What? Your father might have been mowing grass! In my family, for generations people have been playing chess."

Mirza: "*Aji*, come on! You have spent all your life as a chef in Gajiuddin Hyder's kitchen! Today, you are dreaming of royalty. Becoming royal is not a game."

Mir: "Why are you insulting elders? They may have worked as chefs. Here, people have been dining with the Nawab at his dining table!"

Mirza: "Arre! Stop it you chaff-cutter! Don't keep blabbering something."

Mir: "Hold your tongue, or else! I am not in the habit of listening to such words. If someone ever dared to stare at us, we blind him. Are you brave enough?"

Mirza: "You want to check on my valour? Then come on! Let us fight it out here or there."

Mir: "Who is ready here to be suppressed?"

Both the friends removed their swords. It was the time of the Nawabs; everybody carried swords, daggers, knives, etc. Both of them were pleasure-lovers but not cowards. The patriotic feelings in them had vanished- why should one die for the King or the Kingdom? But there was no dearth of personal valour. Both of them fell injured and died after suffering pain. The two of them who could not shed a tear for their emperor now sacrificed their lives to protect their King on the Chess board.

Darkness enveloped. The board was set. It seemed the two Kings on the board sat on their thrones and moarned the death of the two valiant soldiers.

There was pin-drop silence all over. The broken arches, the fallen walls and the dusty pillars of the ruins were all fuming watching the two corpses.

A *Seer*[*] and Quarter of Wheat

This story is an interesting account of the compounding nature of interest charged by the clan of money lenders. This rising interest rates are like the never-ending gut of Goddess Durga, a bane to the society.

There was a small farmer named Shankar in a village. He was a very simple, straightforward and poor farmer. He was a non-nonsense man bothered only about his work. He knew no deception, had no introduction to the surreptious world, had no fear of being cheated, had no knowledge of cheating; if he could get his meal, he ate it; if he did not get, he chewed on some parched grains; if he did not get even that, he drank some water, prayed to Lord Rama and went to bed. But when some guest arrived at his doors, then he had to sacrifice this detached approach. Especially when some saintly person entered his home, he inevitably had to take refuge under worldly ways. He himself could sleep hungry but how could he let the saint, who was a worshipper of God, sleep in hunger?

One evening, a Mahatma came to his doorstep and stayed put. He was a very saintly person, with a radiant persona, donning a silk stole on his shoulders, held a brass *kamandal* (a small spouted pot to hold water), wearing wooden sandals and spectacles. He seemed so much like those saints, who undertook penance, flew to various pilgrim centres and consumed sumpstuous and tasty meals thanks to the offerings of the rich. He had just a little barley flour at home. How could he feed that to this seer? Whatever may have been the importance of barley in the ancient times, the contemporary saints could not digest barley. He was worried as to what he could feed the Mahatma. He finally decided to borrow a little wheat flour from someone but he could not get the same anywhere in the village. All the villagers were after all humans and not *devathas (*divine beings);

[*] Seer: A local measure of weight i.e., about one kilogram

so how could they have things consumed by *devathas?* Fortunately, he could get a little wheat flour from a Brahmin gentleman. He borrowed a *seer* and a quarter of wheat from him and asked his wife to grind it. Mahatma had his lunch and stretched himself and had a good sleep. In the morning, he blessed the hosts and left.

The Brahmin gentleman used to reap the harvest twice a year. Shankar said to himself, 'why should I return that *seer* and a quarter of wheat? Instead I will return a little more than that. He will also understand and I will also be satisfied.' When the Brahmin arrived during the month of *chaithra* (the first month of the lunar calendar), he gave him nearly one and a half *panseers* of wheat. He considered himself fully free of debt and hence did not discuss anything. The Brahmin too never demanded anythingfrom him thereafter. Poor Shankar had no idea that he may have to take a rebirth to make good the *seer* and a quarter of wheat.

Seven years passed by. The Brahmin gentleman became a Maharaj (a reputed money lender), while Shankar had turned into a coolie from a farmer. His younger brother Mangal had separated from him. Together they were farmers, while they became labourers after separation. Shankar wished that the fire of vengeance should never be encouraged by him, but circumstances forced him to do otherwise. The day two hearths started burning within the same house, he wept bitterly. From that day the two brothers would become enemies. When one cries, the other will laugh; when one's house is mourning, there will be celebrations in the other's house; the bondage of love, blood and milk will break forever. He had planted the tree of family honour with great struggle and nurtured it with his blood. Now his heart broke into pieces watching that tree being uprooted. He did not even think of food for seven days. He worked throughout the day in the hot sun of *jeshta* (the first month of the Indian calendar which falls in the summer) and went to bed covering his face. This severe grief and unbearable difficulty boiled his blood and wasted his flesh and bones. He fell ill and could not get out of his bed for months. How should life continue?

He was left with half of five *bighas (*one *bigha* is equivalent to $5/8^{th}$ of an acre of land) of land and one bullock. How can any economical farming be carried with these? Things reached a stage in the end when farming just remained a vocation to save the honour of the family, while the livelihood had to be earned by laboring elsewhere. Seven years went by this way. One day, when Shankar was returning after a hard day's labour, the Brahmin Maharaj stopped him and said, "Shankar, come tomorrow and settle your accounts with the Seed Bank. You owe five and a half *man (*forty *seers* make one *man)* wheat since long but you show no sign of returning the same. Are you planning to swallow it?"

Shankar was shocked and said, "when did I borrow wheat from you to owe five and a half *mans* now. You are forgetting that I do not owe anybody even a *chatank* (the smallest measure of weight) of grain or single paise of debt."

Brahmin: "You are going through this abject hunger only because of this insincerity!"

Saying this, the moneylender reminded Shankar of the one and a quarter *seers* of wheat that he had lent to Shankar seven years ago. Hearing that Shankar was speechless! 'I have farmed so many crops for him in all these years; what has he done for me? Whenever he came to my doors for reading horoscopes or fortelling good and bad, he always received some *dakshina* (remuneration offered to Brahmins). This selfish! He has multiplied one and a quarter *seers* of wheat like incubating an egg and is showing me a demon today, which will devour me. Had he informed me in all these years, I would have weighed the wheat and returned it. Was he keeping quiet all these years just with this intention?' He said, "Maharaj, of course I have not given you wheat with the particular notion of returning what I borrowed; but many times during harvests, I have given you plenty of wheat in *seers.* Now you are all of a sudden demanding five and half *mans*! From where should I get?"

Brahmin: "You might have given me many times and sometimes even four times the worth of my services. There is no account of all that. You have to pay the worth of whatever the account shows. Now there is an outstanding of five and a half *mans* against your name in my books; you can ask anybody to verify. If you return, I will delete your name from my books or otherwise the dues will be rising."

Shankar: “Pandey, why are you bothering a poor man? I have nothing to eat for myself. From where shall I get this quantity of wheat?”

Brahmin: “I don’t care from where you get it from; I will not let go even a *chatank*. If you do not return it here, you shall pay for it in the court of God.”

Shankar shivered. An educated man would have responded, ‘okay, fine! I will pay it up there only; the measure out there will exceed this measure. At least we do not have any evidence of yonder life; then why bother about it?’ But Shankar was not this logical or smart. ‘First of all a debt, that too towards a Brahmin, if left unsettled, I would straight away go to hell.’ This very thought brought goose-pumps in him. He said, “Maharaj, whatever I owe you, I will repay right here. Why carry it forward to God’s court? I am already suffering in this birth, why should I sow thorns for my next birth? But this is not fair. You have made a mountain out of a mole, being a Brahmin, you are not expected to do such a thing. If you had persisted and recovered my dues way back at that moment, there would not have been such a huge burden on my head today. I shall repay surely but you shall pay for this in the court of God.”

Brahmin: “You may be scared of your life up there! Why should I bother? Everybody over there will be my own kith and kin. Saints and *Rishis* are all Brahmins; *Devathas* are anyway Brahmins; if anything goes wrong, they will handle it. So, when are you returning?”

Shankar: “I have nothing with me. I can give you only when I am able to beg or borrow from somebody else.”

Brahmin: “I will not accept this. Already seven years have lapsed; I can wait no more. If you cannot return my wheat, sign the document.”

Shankar: “I have to give anyway either by way of wheat or by signing the document; how will you maintain the account?”

Brahmin: “The market rate is five *seers*, I will consider a quarter *seer* more and open your account.”

Shankar: "When I am repaying anyway, why should I feel guilty of paying you a quarter *seer* less?I shall repay at the market rate."

After making the calculations, the amount worked out to sixty rupees and hence a promissory note for sixty rupees with an interest of 3 rupees per hundred was written. It was mentioned that in case the amount is not returned within a year, then the interest shall be charged at Rs.2.50 per Rs.100/-. Shankar had also to bear eight annas towards the cost of the stamp and four annas towards the cost of the document.

The entire village criticized the Brahmin's action, but never on his face. After all the Maharaj comes in handy for everybody; who could earn his displeasure? Shankar struggled throughout the year. He had taken it as a vow to somehow return the money before the due date. As it is the hearth never burnt during the day and he was managing his hunger on dried pulses. Now, he did not have even that. *Roties* were cooked in the night only for the children. Shankar chewed a little tobacco everyday because he was unable to kick that habit. But now, even that was sacrificed for the sake of his challenge. He dismantled the hookah blower, broke the pot and destroyed the tobacco container. His clothes had already reduced to mere covering on his skin; now even those were sacrificed and bore the novel designs created by nature! He withstood the extreme chillness of winter by lighting fire and heating his body. The fruits of his determination were tastier than his ambition. At the end of the year, he could save eight rupees. He thought of paying the eight rupees to the Brahmin and telling him that he would return the balance as soon as possible. After all it was a matter of just fifteen rupees; won't the Maharaj agree? He went and placed the eight rupees at the feet of the Maharaj. The Pandit was astonished and asked him, "Did you borrow from somebody else?"

Shankar: "No Maharaj; thanks to your blessings, I got a good income."

Brahmin: "But this is just eight rupees?"

Shankar: "Yes Maharaj. You please accept this for now; I will return the balance in two or three months. Then free me of my debt."

Brahmin: "You will be released of the debt only after returning every pie. Go fetch the balance of fifteen rupees now."

Shankar: "Maharaj, please show mercy on me; now I am not able to eat even my night meal! I am right in the village. I shall return definitely some time."

Brahmin: "I do not tolerate this disease! I do not know to talke much too. If I do not get my fifteen rupees right now, interest at the rate of three rupees per hundred will be applicable. You may store your money in your house or leave it here."

Shankar: "Okay. Please keep whatever I have brought. I will go and try to get the balance fifteen rupees by borrowing elsewhere."

Shankar tried all around the village but could not get the money – not because nobody trusted him or nobody had that kind of money but because nobody dared disturb the Pandithji's prey!

A reaction is quite natural to follow an action. When Shankar's year-long concerted penance did not help him free himself of the debt, his tolerance turned into despair. He wondered when eve his hard work of a year could fetch him a saving of just Rs.60/-, what way was he left with to save double that amount. When it was inevitable for him to bear the burden of debt, how does it matter whether it is one or one and a quarter! He lost his zeal and he was tired of work. Hope is the mother of enthusiasm. Hope has strength, power and life. Hope is motive power for the whole world. Shankar lost hope and became depressed. Those necessities that he had stalled throughout the year were no more waiting at the doorstep like beggars but had turned into devils pressing his chest and would not release him without getting satiated. There is a limit even for the number of patches that a piece of cloth can take. Now, if Shankar could make some extra money, he did not save it but bought some clothing or some eatable. He, who just chewed tobacco, now started smoking *ganja* and *charas*. He had no care to save any money as he felt he owed nothing to anybody. Earlier, he went to work even when he was shivering with fever but now he required some pretext to go to work!

Three years passed by this way. The Brahmin Maharaj never made a demand even once. He wanted to make a surprise attack like a clever hunter! It was against his principle to alert the prey in advance! One day, Pandithji called Shankar and showed him the account. Even after deducting sixty rupees that he had paid, he still owed one hundred and twenty rupees as per that. Shankar said, "I will repay this kind of money only in another birth and cannot repay in this birth."

The Brahmin: "I will collect it in this birth only. If not the principal, you have to pay at least the interest."

Shankar: "I have just a bullock left with me; you may take it. I have nothing else."

The Brahmin: "What do I do with a bullock? You have a lot with you that you can give me."

Shankar: "What else are you talking about Maharaj?"

The Brahmin: "You do have something-after all you are left! You go to work somewhere. I do need men to work in my fields. You work in my fields for the interest and return the principal at your convenience. The fact now is that you cannot go to work for anybody else until and unless you clear all your dues to me. You do not have any property. On what guarantee can I forget this huge debt? Who will take the responsibility to ensure that you pay up the monthly interest without fail? When you are not able to pay the interest by working elsewhere, what to say of the principal amount?"

Shankar: "Maharaj, if I work for the interest, what shall I eat?"

The Brahmin: "Your wife is there and you have sons too. Will they sit and relax? As far as I am concerned, I shall give you half a seer of wheat for your meal every day. You shall be provided with a blanket every year and I shall also get a jacket made for you. What else do you need? It is true that others were paying you six annas per day but I do not have such a need. I am employing you to collect my debt."

After thinking deeply for a long time, Shankar said, "Maharaj, this is a lifetime slavery."

The Brahmin: "You may consider it as slavery or employment. I will not spare you forever until you clear my debt. In case you go away, will your son repay. If there is nobody, the matter is different."

There was no place to appeal against this decision. Who will bail out poor labourers? There was no refuge for them to run to. He started working from the next day at the farm of the Brahmin. For the sake of one and a quarter seers of wheat, he had to be bonded for life. If at all there was anything that gave the unfortunate being some happiness, it was the fact that he had the culture of righteousness passed on to him from his previous birth. He had to witness his wife doing things which he had never allowed earlier. His children were longing for food, which he had to helplessly watch in silence. Those grains of wheat never eased from his head like the curse of some God.

Shankar left this heartless world after slogging it out at the Brahmin's farm for twenty years. One hundred and twenty rupees still dangled as his dues. Pandithji did not find it right to bother the poor man in the court of God. After all he was not that unfair or heartless! Instead of that, he caught hold of his son! He has been working at the Brahmin's farm until today. When will be his deliverance or whether it will ever happen, God alone knows!

The Temple and the Mosque

Religious fanatism is a sign of intolerance and does not abstain even from violence. There is no dearth for generous people among Hindus and Muslims but traditionally, when the issue of protection of religion or intrusion arises, the swords are drawn!

Choudhary Isarath Ali was a very generous *Jagirdar.* He was not authoritative but he participated in all social events of both the Muslims and Hindus. He never failed to offer grants in the weddings of Brahmin girls. His relatives were envious of him. On Kirshna Janmashtami, when some miscreants pelted stones, he immediately sent his strong body-guard Bhajan Singh to the spot. Bhajan Singh attacked Choudhary's son Shahid, as he could not recognize him in the darkness. Takur Bhajan Singh then tried to kill himself but Choudhary held back his sword. After hiding the matter for some time, Bhajan Singh surrendered himself before the *Hamid.* Choudhary sat in judgement for the case and saved him from death penalty.

The antagonism between Hindus and Muslims is an endless saga of mutual hatred, everlasting fights over temples and mosques and tolerance and intolerance. Choudhary too was a loyal Muslim. Thus when Bhajan Singh entered the mosque, he considered it as an insult to his religion and was ready to punish him with death but how could he do that to someone whom he had brought up. Bhajan Singh saw his predicament and said, "Choudhary Saab, tomorrow you can get my head fetched from my house. I have committed a crime and I shall accept the punishment."

Choudhary Ishrath Ali was a very powerful *Jagirdar.* His ancestors had served the British Government in many a top posts during the rule of the Shahis. This *Jagir* (land holding) was gifted to them in return for their service. Due to their good governance, they had expanded their landholding extensively and as on date, there was nobody else richer than Choudhary. Whenever the British officers passed by the *Jagir* on official visits, they definitely paid a courtesy visit to Choudhary's farm.However, Choudhary never bowed down and visit any officer on his own, be it the Commissioner himself. He had almost taken a vow never to visit the offices. He also never attended any court of judgement. He felt it was below his dignity to stand in front of some Governor with folded hands and nodding 'Yes Sir' to whatever he says. As far as possible, he avoided involving himself in litigations, even if it meant bringing losses to him. This was definitely the job of advocates, who could make hundred out of one or one out of hundred! He was well versed in Parsee and Arab literature and a strict follower of religious injuctions. He considered it a sin to charge interest, offered prayers five times a day, observed *roza* for all the thirty days during *Ramzaan*and recited *Quran* everyday. But he never got entangled in the religious complexities. He bathed in river Ganga as a daily routine. Whether it rained or snowed, he would wake up at five in the morning without fail and reach the banks of Ganga covering the distance of 2 miles on foot.

While returning, he would fill his silver jug with the water of Ganges and always drank that. He never drank any other water other than that of river Ganges. Even saint or Yogi would not revere the waters of river Ganges to that extent! His entire house and its exteriors would be anointed with cow dung every week. Not just this much. A Pandit performed Durga Puja all the twelve months in his garden. Even emperors used to be astonished with the generosity and devotion that he showed while honouring *Sadhus* and *sansyasis.* It seemed that vows were offered forever. Similarly, nearly hundred and twenty five Muslim Fakirs were fed with the food cooked in the kitchen, on the traditional clothspread. Though he was so generous, there was not a single penny that he owed to anybody. Blessed by his honesty, his cofers swelled up. It was an open rule in his *Jagir* that nobody need take his permission to cut wood in the Government forests for funeral pyre or for performing religious *Yagas* (sacrifices) or for conducting some community festivities or marriages. During the marriage procession of Hindu Assamese, there would definitely be some kind of participation from his side. The money for invitations was ever kept ready in bundles; the dowry for the girls during their marriages was guaranteed; they were offered elephants, horses, *shamianas/pandals,* carriages and palanquins, carpets and beddings, fans, silverware for decoration without any problem on request. His subjects were even ready to give their lives for this generous and successful person.

Choudhary Saheb had a Rajput servant named Bhajan Singh. He was six-foot in height and broad-chested. He could emerge out like an arrow from a crowd of even hundreds. The word 'fear' was unknown to him. Choudhary Saheb had one hundred percent trust in him and he even took him along when he went on Haj. There was no dearth for his enemies. The Zamindars of the neighbouring areas were jealous of his fame and power. They could not ill-treat their subjects because they feared for Choudhary Saheb who was ever ready to interfere and take the side of the helpless poor. But when Bhajan Singh was with him, he had no problem in sleeping even at the doors of his enemies. There were many occasions when he was surrounded by enemies and Bhajan Singh all alone brought him out safely, putting his own life at risk. Nobody would have seen such a brave person who could jump into fire! Whenever he went out and did not return home on time, Choundhary Saheb doubted that he might be fighting with somebody. He was like a domesticated ram which would definitely run to fight with some other ram or sheep, immediately on being unchained. There was nobody in the three worlds except Choudhary Saheb, in Bhajan Singh's mind. Call him the emperor or master or God – Choudhary Saheb was everything to him.

Muslims were jealous of Choudhary Saheb. They felt he had turned away from their religion. How could they understand such a strange philosophy of life? How could a true Muslim drink the waters of river Ganga, show hospitality to Hindu saints and arrange for Durga puja? There was enemity cooking up against him amongst the Mullahs and preparations were being made to attack the Hindus. Finally it was decided that on Janmastami, the temples shall be attacked and Hindus be defeated and taught a lesson that it was their foolishness to be roaming around happily depending upon the strength of Choudhary Saheb. What could Choudhary Saheb after all do? If he rose to protect the Hindus, then he would also be taken to task so that all the Hinduism in him would be ousted out.

It was a dark night. Krishna's birthday was being celebrated in all big households of the Thakurs. One old shriveled gentleman was singing the *alaap* in *drupad*style with a *tambura* in his hand and many devotees were waiting with varieties of cymbals in their hands, for the old man to stop so that they start singing. Bhandary was preparing the *prasad*. People had gathered in hundreds to watch the fun.

All of a sudden, a troop of Muslims arrived there with lathies in their hands and started pelting stones on the temple. People started shouting, "where are the stones coming from? Who is pelting them?" Some people went out of the temple to check out. Muslims were lying in ambush and started wielding their lathies immediately on seeing them. The Hindus had nothing but their scymbals in their hands. Some of them went into the temple and hid themselves while some of them ran helter-skelter. There was pandemonium all over the place.

Choudhary Saheb too heard about this. He told Bhajan Singh, "Thakur, go find out what this din is all about. Go and try driving sense into those hooligans. If they do not yield, you may give a few slaps but ensure that there is no bloodshed."

Thakur was grinding his teeth, hearing about the pandemonium. He was controlling his anger with a heavy heart. As soon as he heard this order, he felt that his wish had been granted. Holding the enemy-destroying lathi on his shoulder, he swiftly arrived at the temple. Muslims had created a huge disturbance there at the temple. Running behind many a Hindu, they had entered the temple and they were indulging in destroying glass articles there.

Thakur's eyes bled and his blood boiled. Challenging the hooligans in a loud voice, Thakur entered the temple and started beating them up. He was facing around fifty opponents all alone but what to speak of the roaring tiger! He drove courage out of many and killed many others. He lost his senses in his anger and cared little of who died and who survived. God knows from where he got all that strength. He felt that some divine power was assisting him. It seemed Bhagwan Krishna himself was saving him. In the struggle to protect *Dharma*(justice/righteousness), miracles happen through humans.

After Thakur left, Choudhary Saheb started fearing that he should not end up killing people and he followed him to the temple. He saw that there was total commotion and heard cries of pain. Some hooligans were running for their lives in fright, while some lay dead, while some were wriggling in pain. He was about to beckon Thakur, when suddenly a man came running and fell in front of him. Choudhary Saheb immediately recognized him and the entire world turned dark to him. That was his only son-in-law Shahid Hussainm, who was the heir to his entire property.

Choudhary quickly held him and shouted, “Thakur, come here. Get a lantern, a lantern quickly. This is my Shahid....Oh!”

Thakur’s limbs went cold. He came out with a lantern. Yes! It was indeed Shahid Hussain. His skull was broken and blood oozing out from his head.

Choudhary was beating his breast and said, “Thakur, you have put out my own flame.”

Thakur started shivering and said, “Master, God knows I did not recognize him.”

Choudhary: “No. I am not blaming you. Nobody has the right to trespass into a temple. It is only sad that the lineage has been obliterated and that too at your hands! You would always risk even your life for my sake and now God has chosen you as an instrument to destroy me!”

Choudhary kept uttering such words and weeping hoarsely. Thakur was shaken with remorse and sorrow. He wouldn’t have felt this bad even if he had lost his own son. ‘Ah! I have destroyed my master’s life with my own hands! I have uprooted the base of the household of the person for whose sake I would rather shed my blood instead of sweat, the person who is just not my master but my idol and on whose orders I am ready to jump into fire!’ He turned into a poisonous snake to his own master! In a heavy tone, he said, “Sarkar, who could be more unfortunate than me? I have defaced myself.”

Saying this, Thakur removed the knife from his waist band. He was just about to pierce his chest and wash away the stain of his blemish with his blood, when Choudhary Saheb quickly snatched the knife from him and said, "What are you doing? Come to senses! This is all the game of fate. You need not blame yourself. Whatever was destined by God has happened. Even if I myself had entered into the temple and insulted the God and you had murdered me, I would have pardoned you. No sin is worse than insulting somebody's faith. Though at this moment my heart is being torn apart and this grief can even take away my life, God knows I carry no grudge against you. Had I been in your place, I too would have done the same thing, be it my own master's son. My family may bombard me with taunts; my grief-stricken daughter may demand that I avenge her loss; the entire Muslim community may bay for my blood; I may earn the titles of heretic and apostate; why, someyoung zealotfrom my faith may well resolve to execute me for this transgression. Yet I will stand my ground! Flee forthwith under the cover of this darkness and hide yourself in some obscure shack in my territory. Look—several Muslims are heading this way, including some from my own family. Hurry, run!"

Bhajan Singh remained hidden in Choudhary Saheb's territory for a whole year. He was hounded by the vengeful Muslims on one side, and by the police on the other. But Choudhary always kept him protected. Choudhary withstood the taunts from his community, rejection from his family, harassment from the police, the threats from the *Mullahs* and yet never gave an inkling about Bhajan Singh's whereabouts! He did not want to give up such a loyal and faithful servant to the ruthless clutches of law during his lifetime.

The shelters and shacks in Choudhary's territory were raided many times. The Mullahs tried extracting information through the servants, uncles and girls of the household but Choudhary kept Thakur protected like his favours.

Thakur felt stifled that Choudhary had to put up with so much of trouble in order to save his life. Time and again he felt like telling him, "please hand me over to the police." But Choudhary Saheb kept pressurizing him to keep himself under cover.

It was winter time. Choudhary Saheb was touring around his territory. He spent very limited time in his house. This was the only way he could save himself from the sharp tongues of the family members. He was lying down after his dinner, when Bhajan Singh appeared in front of him. His face had changed so much that Choudhary was shocked. Thakur inquired, "Is Sarkar fine?"

Choudhary- "Yes, by God's grace. I cannot even recognize you. Where are you coming from right now?"

Thaku- "Master, I can hide no more. With your permission, I would go and surrender at the court. Whatever is destined shall prevail. You are going through so much of stress because of me, which I am unable to bear."

Choudhary- "No Thakur! Not when I am still alive! I cannot bring myself to cast into the fire knowingly.The police will fabricate the testimony as they please and I will have to give you up freely. You have borne grave dangers for my sake. If I cannot do even this much for you, then don't tell me anything."

Thakur – "Sarkar, if somebody somewhere ......"

Choudhary- "Don't you bother about that. Until and unless the Lord wishes, nobody can cause any harm to me. Now, you get away from here. It is unsafe."

Thakur- "I heard people have started avoiding you."

Choudhary- "It is good that enemies keep away from me. But whatever impression has got into Thakur's mind will never erase. This meeting has strengthened this fact even further. You are forced to wander like this because of me. Who is here to call your own? Whoever wants can come and attack you. To hell with the life that I am leading thus!"

Thakur arrived at the office of the Zilla head early in the morning. Saheb enquired, "Were you in the hiding as per Choudhary's wish?"

Thakur- "No Saheb, out of the fear for my life."

Choudhary Saheb was speechless when he heard this. What now? If the case is not contested, it would be difficult to save Thakur. But if he contested, then there will be an uproar in the Muslim community. *Fatwas*will emerge from all sides. The Muslims had resolved that they would send Thakur to the gallows. Funds were being collected. The *Mullahs* made appeals for donations in the Masjids and went around with sacks. The case got coloured as a communal case. The Muslim advocates found an opportunity to earn fame through this case. People from neighbouring areas started arriving to participate in the *jihad*.

Choudhary Saheb decided to contest the case, come what may. He found Thakur innocent in the eyes of law and he had no fear in saving an innocent person from the jaws of law. He set out of his home and settled down in the city.

He fought the case wholeheartedly for six months. He spent money like water and fought fiercely like a storm. He did everything that he had never done earlier nor did later. He flattered the officials; carried loads for the advocates; paid visits to the *hakims* and managed to free Thakur from the clutches of law. There was commotion all over the place. Everybody was shocked on hearing about this. This is called nobility! He had saved his servant from the gallows!

But the natural enimity between the two communities viewed this good deed from a different angle- while the Muslims went red in anger, the Hindus were highly delighted! Muslims felt this person had given up his religious affinity. The Hindus thought that the time had arrived for them to sanctify him. The *Mullahs* fervently appealed for religious revolutionwhile the Hindus too called for unity. The Muslim fervor in the Muslims and the *Hindutva*in the Hindus got awakened. Thakur too lost his footing in this deluge. Being naturally whimsical, he became the leader of the Hindus. He had not offered even a glass of water to Lord Shiva in his lifetime but was now prepared to raise arms for the sake of Gods and Goddesses. If he could not find any Muslim to be corrected, he ended up sanctifying a few *chamars* (low caste). This reflected upon the other servants of Choudhary Saheb too. Those Muslims who had never bothered to even go past a Masjid now offered prayers five times a day and those Hindus who never peeped into a temple earlier now started performing *Sandhya Vandan* (a religious ritual of prayer to Sun God and other Gods) twice a day.

The Hindu population was denser in the locality. To top it, Bhajan Singh, who was well known for his physical strength and valour, became their leader. Before this, though the Muslims were smaller in number, wielded power over Hindus because the Hindus were not united. But now that the Hindus too became united, the minority group of Muslims was no match for them.

One more year passed by and once again arrived *Janmashtami.* The Hindus had not forgotten their defeat of the previous year. Preparations were on secretly. Devotees started gathering at the temple right from early morning. Everbody carried a *lathi* while a few had even hidden knives in their waists. The idea of kicking up a fight by provocation was finalized. Never before had there been a procession on this occasion. But today, preparations were on to take out a grand procession.

The lamps had burnt out. The evening *namaz*(prayers) was being offered at the Masjids. The procession set out. Elephant, horses, flags, posters, cymbals and drums were all there. Bhajan Singh was leading the procession exhibiting his strength along with his fellow gymnasts.

The procession neared the Jama Masjid. The gymnasts held up their *lathis* and everybody got ready. Even the few who had strayed away here and there came and joined the procession. They whispered something amongst themselves. The drum beats got louder. The people cheered in loud voices. The procession now was right in front of the Masjid.

Just then a Muslim came out of the Masjid and said, "please stop playing the music. It is prayer time."

Bhajan Singh- Music will not stop.

Muslim – You have to stop it.

Bhajan Singh- Why don't you stop your *namaz*?

Muslim- Don't brag around on the strength of Choudhary Saheb. This pride will soon be snubbed.

Bhajan Singh- You may swell on the strength of Choudhary Saheb! Here we trust our own strength. This is an issue of our religion.

Meanwhile, a few more Muslims came out and requested for the music to be stopped but it was only getting louder. The issue got more serious. A *moulvi* called Bhajan Singh an infidel. Thakur immediately held on to his beard. What could happen thereafter? Warring people came on to the scene and a fight broke out. Thakur made loud war calls and entered the Masjid. A fierce fight continued inside there. It was not clear as to who had an upper hand. The Muslims claimed that they beat the Hindus black and blue while the Hindus claimed that they gave the Muslims such a beating that they would never dare to raise their heads again. But everybody was talking about one thing and that was Thakur Bhajan Singh's unworldly valour. The Muslims said that they would not have spared anybody but for the presence of Bhajan Singh and the Hindus said that Bhajan Singh was indeed an incarnation of a great warrior. Nobody could face the powerful blows that Bhajan Singh gave with his *lathi.*

The celebrations concluded. Choudhary Saheb was enjoying a round of *hukka* in his *Deewankhana*. His face was red, eye brows raised and eyes were burning with anger. 'Lord's abode was defiled'. This thought haunted him and churned his mind.

'Lord's abode dirtied! Did the hooligans not have a field outside to fight? Such bloodbath in the holy house of God! Such an insult to a Masjid! Both a temple and a masjid are abodes of Gods. When a Muslim deserves a severe punishment for defiling a temple, does not a Hindu too deserve an equally severe punishment for defiling a masjid? And Thakur committed this sin! He murdered my son-in-law for the same offence. Had I known he would commit such an offence, I would have allowed him to go to the gallows. Why did I face so much of insult, ill-fame and tension for his sake? Thakur is my loyal servant. He has saved my life many times and is ready to shed blood for my sake. But today he has defiled God's abode and he has to be punished for that. What is the punishment? Hell! The only punishment that I can think of for this grave offence is death. Whoever has defiled Lord's abode has insulted the Lord himself! Insult!'

Presently, Thakur Bhajan Singh appeared in front of him.

Choudhary Saheb looked at him angrily and said, "You entered a masjid?"

Bhajan Singh – "Sarkaar, the *moulvis* attacked us."

Choudhary- “Answer my question. Did you enter the masjid?”

Bhajan Singh- “When they pelted stones at us from inside the masjid, we entered the masjid to catch them.”

Choudharty- “Do you know that the masjid is the abode of the Lord?”

Bhajan Singh: “Yes. I do know. Don’t I know even that?”

Choudhary: “Masjid is as holy an abode as a temple is for the God.”

Bhajan Singh did not retort to this.

Choudhary: “If some Muslim is stupid in trespassing into a temple, a Hindu too is stupid to trespass into a masjid.”

Bhajan Singh could not reply anything to this remark too. He had never ever seen Choudhary Saheb so furious.

Choudhary: “You killed my son-in-law but I fought for you. Do you know why I did so? Because I felt my son-in-law deserved the punishment that you had meted out to him. Even if you had killed my own son or even me for such an offence, I would not have demanded an eye for an eye. Today you have committed the same offence. Had some Muslim sent you to hell at the masjid, I would have been really happy. But you have escaped from there shamelessly. Do you think the God will not punish you for your commission? It is the Lord’s order that whoever insults Him shall be beheaded. This is the duty of every Muslim. Isn’t a thief not a thief if he escapes punishment? Do you agree or not that you have insulted God?”

Thakur could not deny his offence. His nearness to Choudhary blinded his fanatism. He said, “Yes Saheb. I have committed that offence.”

Choudhary: “Are you ready to face the same punishment that you handed over for the same offence?”

Thakur: “I had not killed your son-in-law knowingly.”

Choudhary: “Had you not killed him, I would have killed him with my own hands. Do you understand? Now I shall avenge you for insulting the God. Tell me whether you want justice through the court or from me. The court may just jail you for a few days. I will kill you. You are my friend. But I don't care. Only God knows how much it hurts me. But I will kill you. This is my Lord's order."

Saying this, Choudhary Saheb stood in front of Thakur with his sword drawn out. It was a strange scene. An old man in grey hair and bent back stood with his sword in front of a giant. Thakur could easily oppose the old man just with his *lathi.*But he just bowed. He was filled with reverence for Choudhary. He had never imagined that Choudhary was so staunch a believer in his faith. He had probably mistaken that he was a Hindu by heart. He could never think of revenge or violence against that master, who had saved him from the gallows. He was courageous and plain hearted. At this moment, he was not angry but was filled with repentence. Faith beckoned him to kill but decency asked him to let go. There was a struggle between faith and righteousness.

Thakur saw Choudhary's instability. He majestically said, "Master, your compassion will not let you raise your arm against me. You cannot kill the servant whom you have brought up. This head is yours. You saved it, now you can take it. After all it was your treasure which lay with me till now. You will get this treasure. You may send someone in the morning and get it fetched. If I hand it over here, you may feel uncomfortable. Who will know if I die at home? Please pardon me for my shortcomings."

Manthra (Panecea)

It is common in the society to convert people or stop conversion. This is the story of Leeladhar Choube, who goes down south to stop conversion, gets avenged but then gets saved from the same people who looked down upon him. It describes the odd behavior of a society. Finally, what prevails is humanitarian consideration above all!

There was magic in Leeladhar Choube's tongue. The moment he gets on to the podium and starts his oratory, the souls of the fans get satisfied and they get intoxicated with a feeling of compassion. There was very less of substance or ornamental language in Choubeji's talks but the effect of repeating things was not bad. In fact his words acted like the repeated strokes of a sledgehammer and created the desired effect on the audience. It is hard to believe but the listeners say that he has learnt by rote just one speech and keeps repeating the same word to word in every meet, in a different style. The chief feature of his talk was glorification of caste system. Immediately on beginning his talk, he would praise India's ancient glory and the eternal fame of our ancestors and attract the listeners. Thus goes, "Gentlemen, who would not shed tears on hearing about the story of our destruction? When we recollect our ancient glory, we start wondering whether we are the same or have changed! The one who challenged a lion yesterday goes in search of a bow to face a mouse today! There is a limit to this path. Why go that far? Just go the times of Maharaj Chandragupta. A Greek historian writes that in those times, the doors were never locked; he never heard of any thievery; there was no sign of prostitution; documents were yet to be invented; dealings of lakhs took place based on just obscure bits of paper; the judicial staff members literally had no work to do! Nobody died young in those days. (applause). Yes. In those days, no man died young. It was very rare and impossible for a son to die before his father.

Today you can find very many parents who are burdened with the death of their offspring. It is no more that India but has been fully destroyed."

This was Choubeji's style. He aroused communal feelings of self respect in people by singing the glory of the rich past and highlighting the bad state and destruction of the present age. Mainly because of his this capacity, he was counted among the leaders. He was especially considered as a helmsman of Hindu gatherings. There was no other orator in the Hindu Sabha who was so enthusiastic, so able and so strong in morality. He had devoted his entire life for the sake of the Hindu Sabha. He had no personal wealth; at least that was the impression among his followers; but he had the invaluable qualities of valour, boldness and intellect in abundance, which he had totally dedicated for the cause of Hindu Sabha. Chastity was his life. According to him, the ups and downs and life and death wholly depended upon this question. He felt there was no other way than purity for the resurrection of Hinduism. The panacea for all the moral, physical, mental, social, economic and religious illnesses of the religion lay in this revolution and he worked hard whole-heartedly towards this goal.He was an expert in collecting donations. God had blessed him with the ability to extract oil even from stones! He would rag misers with such sharp vocabulary that they would learn lessons of a lifetime! As far as this matter was concerned he used all the four means viz.,*sam, dam, dand* and *bhed* (prayer, spending some funds, punishment and disunion). He went to the extent of even justifying robbing and burglary for the welfare of the nation!

It was summer time. He was planning to visit some cool hill station so that his twin purposes of touring as well collecting funds would be served. When he wished to travel, he planned a trip as a deputation along with a few friends, never mind if he manages to collect just a thousand rupees as donation out of which he would end up spending nearly fifty percent for himself and his friends. What's the harm in it? After all the Hindu Sabha gets something. But for his efforts, the Sabha would have not got even that much. Panditji had planned to go along with his group of friends. Since the time this cleansing project was taken up, the economic status of the Sabha which was dismal, had improved a lot.

But how can the religious activists dream of enjoying the bliss of a peaceful home? They are after all born to be roaming around like vagabonds all their lives. The news arrived about the commotion created by the religious fanatics of Madras state. Entire villages of Hindus were being converted into Muslim villages. The Mullahs had begun their project of mass conversion very enthusiastically. If the Hindu Sabha did not take any step to stop this immediately, then the entire State may not be left even with a single Hindu and not one of those tuftbearers would be found! There was uproar in the Hindu Sabha. An emergent meet was held and the issue was brought to the notice of the leaders. After a lot of thoughtful discussions, it was decided to hand over this responsibility to Choubeji. It was decided to request him to immediately proceed to Madras State and work for reconversion of the converts. No sooner than he was entrusted this job, Choubeji cancelled his trip to the mountains and started preparations to go to Madras State, as he had already pledged his life for the cause of the Hindu Sabha. The Minister of the Hindu Sabha pleaded with tearful eyes, "Maharaj, this burden can be borne by none other than you. The Almighty has endowed you with such a capability. There is no person other than you in this vast country who can be of use at such a serious adversity. Please show mercy on the sorry state of the religion." Choubeji could not reject this request. Immediately a group of *sevaks* under the leadership of Panditji set out. Hindu Sabha hosted them a very grand feast to see them off. A benevolent rich man donated a purse to Choubeji and thousands of people turned up at the railway station to see them off. There was no necessity of writing a chronicle of the journey. At every station, they were warmly welcomed by *sevaks*. In many places, they received purses. The aristrocrats of Ratlam donated a *shamiana* (a tent house). The donors of Baroda donated them a motor vehicle so that the *sevaks* need not take the trouble walking all around. By the time the team reached Madras, besides a considerable amount of money, they had collected many a useful thing. The Hindu Sabha put up the *shamiana* in an open ground far away from the populated areas. The national flag was hoisted on top of the tent house. The *sevaks* wore their uniforms. The rich people of Madras sent them the grocery and tents were pitched. The camp was spoken about on all four sides of the city, as though it was the camp of a king. It was eight in the night. A tent of the *sevak dal* was working near a *basthi* of untouchables with the help of gas lanterns. There was thousands of people gathered there, most of whom were untouchables. A separate hemp was spread for them. The upper caste Hindus were sitting on carpets. Panditji's touching oration was on- "You are the children of those saints who could create a new world below the sky, before whose justice, intellect and analytical skills, the entire world bows its head today.

At that moment, an old untouchable man rose up and enquired, "Are we also the children of the same saints?"

Leeladhar – "Undoubtedly! The same blood of the saints flows through your veins too. You may be looked down upon by today's heartless, narrow-minded, cruel and dumb Hindu society. You are no less a Hindu than anybody else who thinks he is of upper status."

The old man – "Why doesn't your Sabha work for our upliftment?"

Leeladhar- "Hindu Sabha was founded very recently and we are proud about our achievements within such a short time. The Hindu religion has just woken up from deep slumber after centuries. Now that time is nearing when in this country, no Hindu will look down upon another fellow Hindu and everybody treats everybody else like their own brethren. Shriramchandra had embraced a hunter and eaten the same fruit that the old Shabari had eaten…."

Old man- "When you too are the sons of the same saints, why then this discrimination?"

Leeladhar- "Because we have become corrupt. We have drowned ourselves in ignorance and have forgotten those great saints."

Old man- "Now that you have woken up, will you come and have a meal along with us?"

Leeladhar- "I have no problem."

Old man- "Will you give your daughter in marriage to my son?"

Leeladhar- "Until there is a change in your lifestyle, until there is a change in your food habits, we cannot have marital relations with your clan. Stop eating non-vegetarian food, stop drinking liquor, educate yourselves. Only then can you mingle with the upper caste Hindus."

Old man- "I have seen hundreds of the so-called Brahmins who are drunk night and day, who do not eat even morsel of food without meat and who cannot read a single letter with whom you sit on par and have meals. You have no objection in having even marital relations with them. When you yourself are still ignorant, how can you uplift us? You are still filled with ego. Go and first cleanse your soul first. Our upliftment is impossible for you. The scar of lower caste can never be erased as long as we remain Hindus. However educated, however cultured we may become, you will always consider us as low-caste only. The souls of Hindus are dead and ego has replaced the same. Today, we are going towards the God, whose followers are ready to embrace us. They do not tell us to come back after changing our culture. They beckon us as we are, whether good or bad. If you are of upper caste, remain so. We need not fly to reach you."

Leeladhar- "I am surlprised to hear this from a son of a saint! Caste system was introduced by those saints themselves. How can you abolish that?"

The old man: "Do not defame those saints. All these humbug doctrines are framed by people like you. You say we consume licquor but you are bootlickers of drunkards. You quote our meat-eating habit for discriminating us but you become humble in the presence of beef-eaters. Isn't it because they are stronger than you? Today if I become a monarch, you will not hesitate to stand with folded hands in front of me! In your religion, the one who is strong is of upper caste while the weaker one belongs to the lower caste. Is this your religion?" Saying this, the old man left the place and a few more people also stood up. Finally only Choubeji and his few teammates were left on the stage and it seemed like the show was over and the sounds were reverberating all around. The religious fanatics had been planning to somehow drive these people right from the day they heard about their arrival. Choubeji was known far and wide. They knew that if he settles down here, all their efforts will go in vain. He should somehow not be allowed to settle down. The Mullahs thought of various plans. After a lot of thinking, discussion, wrangling and argument, it was decided that he should be assassinated. What was the dearth for men to carry out such acts? The doors of heaven would be open to such persons, the angels will take away all their sins, the fairies will adorn their eyes with the dust of these persons, the messenger of God will bless them with prosperity, *Khuda*'s favourite Karim will embrace them and say, 'you are my dear friends.' Two healthy and strong young men immediately took upon themselves this holy task.

It was past ten in the night. There was total silence in the Hindu Sabha camp. Choubeji was sitting all alone in his tent and writing a letter to the minister of Hindu Sabha – 'the biggest need over here is that of money. Rupee, rupee and rupee! Send us as much as you can. Send people on deputation, scramble the pockets of the rich and beg them for funds. These unfortunate beings can never be uplifted without funds. How can the Hindu Sabha win the trust of these people that they care for their welfare, unless we start a few schools, establish a few health centres and open a few libraries for their sake? If I get even half of the kind of money that the missionaries are spending, I can bring victory to the Hindu religion. Mere empty speeches will be of no use. Nobody can remain alive merely on blessings!'

Just then he heard some footsteps and got startled. He lifted his eyes and found two young men standing in front of him. He doubtfully inquired, "who are you? What can I do for you?"

Reply- "we are the angels of Isreal. We have come to capture your soul. Isreal has thought of you."

Panditji was a very strong man and if he minded he could have just pushed the two of them down. Every morning he consumed three measures of *mohanbhog*(a kind of sweet dish made of concentrated milk) and two *seers* (measures) of milk for breakfast. At noon time he added nearly a measure of ghee to his *dal* and chewed milk-white *bhang*(a kind of intoxicant) in which he added a *seer* full of butter and half a *seer* of almond, in the evening. He never failed to eat his supper in the night because he did not eat anything until early morning! To top it all, he never walked a step! He only had to find a palanquin, he felt as though his bed at home was flying! If nothing, he would always find a two-wheeled carriage drawn by a horse or bullock. But there were a few men of Kashi, who owned these carriages who would say their carriages were engaged the moment they saw him! He was such a person who could tire the wrestler on top of him merely by lying tenderly on the arena! At times of adversities when he had to act briskly with agility, he was like a tortoise exposed on sand! He stole a look at the door. There was no way he could escape. At that moment bravery overwhelmed him. The peak of utmost fear is dare-devilry! He reached out for his baton and roared, "get away from here."

He had yet to complete the sentence when he was attacked with *lathis.* Panditji fell swoon. The enemies came closer and looked at him. There was no sign of life. They thought their task was done. They had no plans to loot. But when there was nobody watching them, what could stop them from laying their hands on stuff? Whatever they could grab, they took them and left.

Early in the morning, when the old man set out, there was absolute silence all over. There were neither men nor any sign of humankind. The tents had all vanished! He was astonished as to what that magic was! Just in a night everything had vanished like Allauddin's palace! He could find not a single gentleman, who gobbled *mohanbhog* in the morning and pounding *bhang* in the evening. He went closer to the tent in which Leeladhar stayed and peeped in. His heart sank! Panditji was lying on the floor like a corpse. Flies were buzzing over his face. Blood had clot on his hair, which seemed like an artiste's brush dipped in red paint. His clothes were wet with blood. He thought Panditji's teammates had beaten him up and escaped from the scene. Just then he heard Panditji moaning. He was still alive. The old man immediately ran to his *basthi,* brought a few men from there and fetched Panditji to his house. The wounds were dressed. The old man sat beside Panditji night and day, while his family members nursed him. The other residents too pitched in their mite. There was nobody of poor Panditji's 'own' to take care of him. 'Whether he considers us his own or strangers, we are the only ones here. After all he came this far only for our upliftment. Otherwise, why would he have to come here?' Many times, when Panditji had fallen ill while at home, even his own family members had not nursed him with this much of care. Not only that particular household, but the entire village was at his service. Serving the guests was a part of their culture/faith. The selfishness of civilization had not choked that noble feeling. Till this day, the villager who knew to extract the venom of the snake with his spells, runs miles even in the cloudy pitch dark nights of the months of *magh-pushya* (the cold winter months) to do his duty. He does not demand for double fees or conveyance. The old man cleaned up Panditji's urine and shit with his hands and put up with his irritants. He collected milk from fellow villagers and fed him. There was not a bit of change in his temper. If his family members showed even a bit of negligence in his absence, he reprimanded them on his return.

After a month, Panditji became fit to walk around and it was then that he realized how much those people had helped him. 'These were the people who saved me from the jaws of death. Otherwise, how long would have I taken to die?' He realized that the people whom he considered as downtrodden and had come with the mission of uplifting them, were much more cultured than himself. 'Had I come across such a wounded person, I would have just admitted him in a hospital and taken pride in my duty-consciousness. I would have felt that I had made the great mythological saint Dadhichi, who sacrificed his life in the service of Gods or Raja Harishchandra, who sacrificed his everything for the sake of truth, proud of me!' He was filled with blessings for these children of God. Three months passed by. Neither the Hindu Sabha nor Panditji's family made any enquiry about Panditji. There were touching obituaries in the Sabha's journal praising him for all his contributions to the Sabha and funds were being collected to raise a memorial in his name. Family members were in deep grief. Panditji was getting stronger by the day eating ghee and drinking milk. The blood stains and scars vanished from his face and he put on weight. The rural atmosphere did such wonders to his body that even those kilos of cream and butter could not do! Of course he was not as fit as he was earlier but definitely his agility and briskness doubled. There was no sign of the lazy obesity. New life seemed to be flowing in him.

Winter had set in and Panditji was making preparations to get back home. Just then plague broke out and three villagers, including the old Choudhary, fell ill. The families were set on running away from there, leaving the afflicted to their fate. It was the practice there to leave back those patients, whom they considered as smitten by Devi's ire. To save them was to earn the enemity of the Gods and if they do that, where can they go? How could they dare to snatch away the lives chosen by the God? The people wanted to take Panditji too along with them but he did not go. He decided to stay back in the village and take care of the ill. How could he desert that soul which had saved him from the clutches of death, in such a condition? Gratitude had awoken his soul. On the third day, when Choudhary regained his consciousness and saw Panditji near him, he said, "Maharaj, why did you come here? God has beckoned for me. I cannot stay back under any circumstances. Why are you putting your life in danger? Please have mercy on me and leave immediately." But this had no effect on Panditji. He would go to all the three patients by turn, feeling their ganglions or reading out stories from the Puranas for them. Grocery and vessels lay abandoned. Panditji cooked porridge and fed the patients. When the patients went off to sleep in the night and the entire village looked deserted, Panditji could see scary insects. His heart-beats would get louder and faster. But he never got the thought of leaving the place. He had decided that he would either save these people or sacrifice his life for them. When there was no improvement in the condition of the patients even after his whole-hearted nursing, he got worried. The city was twenty miles away from that village. There was no sign of trains. The roads were arduous and there was no traveler. What would be the fate of these patients if left on their own? Helpless Panditji was perplexed. In the end, on the evening of the fourth day, he walked all alone to the city and reached there by ten in the night. He found it very difficult to get medicines from the hospital. The hospital authorities were fleecing innocent villagers and selling the medicines at exhorbitant rates. Why would they part with such medicines for free to Panditji? The doctor told the Munshi, "the medicines are not ready." Panditji humbly requested, "Sarkar, I have come from a very long distance. If I do not get the medicines, they will all die."

Munshi got irritated and said, "why are you eating my head? He has already told you the medicines are not ready and it is impossible to prepare them at such short notice." Panditji pleaded very politely,

"Sarkar, I am a Brahmin. I bless that your children become immortal. Please show mercy. May your sympathy prevail!

How can corrupt workers be merciful? After all they are slaves of money. The more Panditji flattered him, the more annoyed was he getting. Panditji had never been that submissive ever in his life. He had not a penny on him. Had he known it would be so difficult to get the medicines, he would have borrowed money from the villagers before he came. He stood helplessly unable to think of any idea. The doctor came out of the bungalow. Panditji immediately fell at the doctor's feet and pleaded with compassion, "Oh! Saviour, three men in my house are suffering from plague. I am very poor Sarkar, please dispense some medicine." Everyday such poverty-stricken people visited the doctor. People falling at his feet or crying helplessly was nothing new to him. If such pleading words could arouse compassion in him, he would have stocked a large quantity of medicines! How could he put up such a show? But whatever may be the evil thoughts inside his mind, he spoke very sweetly. He released his feet from Panditji's grip and asked him, "where are the patients?"

Panditji- "Sarkar, they are at home. How can I get them this far?"

Doctor- "Patients are at home and you have come for the medicines? What a joke! How can I dispense medicines without examining the patients?"

Panditji realized his mistake. In fact without examining the patients, how can the illness be identified? But it was not easy for him to fetch three patients this far. If the villagers cooperated with him, *dolis* (a kind of closed litter in which people would be carried; somewhat like a stretcher for carrying patients) could be arranged. But he had no hope of getting any sort of help from the villagers; he had to manage on his own. How will they help? They are turning into his enemies. The villagers were scared that some calamity will strike them if they earn the wrath of the Gods. Had it not been Panditji but somebody else daring such acts, they would have killed him. But since they had started loving Panditji, they let him be. Hearing the doctor's words, Panditji had no guts to say anything more but he gathered courage and asked him, "Sarkar, can nothing be done now?

Doctor-"You cannot get any medicines from the hospital. Maybe I can spare some medicines at a cost."

Panditji- "How much would the medicines cost Sarkar?"

Doctor said the medicines would cost ten rupees and said that these medicines would be more effective than the ones he could get from the hospital because they stock old medicines. He said, "Poor people come and take those medicines. The ones destined to die, while some fortunate ones survive. What does it matter to us? But the medicines I give you will be original ones." Ten rupees! At this time those ten rupees seemed like ten lakh rupees to Panditji.

He used to squander away ten rupees on *bhang* in a day! But at this time, he was in dire need of every penny. He had no hope of borrowing such a money from anybody. Yes. There was one possibility. By begging, maybe he could get a few pennies but there was no way of getting ten rupees in such a short time. He stood there for half-an-hour, totally perplexed. Other than beggary he got no other idea but he had never begged anytime in his life. He had collected donations and collected thousands of rupees in no time. But that was a different story. There was an honour in collecting funds as a protector of religion, servant of castes and the one who worked for the upliftment of Dalits. He was obliging the donors there but here pleading for money like beggars, he had to be submissive and bear the insults. Some will say, 'Arre, you look fit and fine, why can't you work? Aren't you ashamed of begging?' Some will say, 'Go cut some grass and get it for me; I will pay you good wages'. Some may not believe that he is a Brahmin. If he could get a silk *dhoti* and white silk *kurta* with an orange *dupatta* he could go in disguise to beg. He could pose as an astrologer and trap some wealthy *Seth*. He was a professional in this art. But where were the things for all that? Even if he had to buy the clothings, he was a pauper now. Our brains too fail us in adversities! If he stood in a ground and tendered an interesting lecture, he may have won a few hearts. But in the present state of his mind, he could not think of such things. He could exhibit the skill of his tongue on a well-decorated stage, standing in front of a bedecked table. Who would listen to his speech in such a bad state? People might think some mad man is barking. But the time was running out and he had not much time to think. If evening set in, he would find it difficult to get back by night. Then he could not imagine in what state the patients would be! He could wait no longer indecisively! Whatever be the insults that he may have to face, however much he might be ignored, begging was the only option. He went to the market place and stood near a shop but could not muster courage to beg.

The shopkeeper asked, "what do you want?"

Panditji inquired, "how much does rice cost?"

But he became a bit more cautious when he went to the second shop. Sethji was sitting on his *gaddi* (a cushioned seat). Panditji stood before him and recited a verse from the Bhagawat Gita. The Seth was astonished on hearing his clear pronunciation and sweet voice and asked him, "where are you from?"

Panditji- "I am coming from Kashi."

Saying this Panditji spoke about all the features of the religion and gave a very lucid explanation of the verse to the Seth, who was spellbound. He said, "Maharaj, please visit my house and make it holy." Any selfish man would have immediately grabbed this opportunity happily but Panditji had to return today. "No Sethji, I have no time."

Seth- "Maharaj, I have at least to do that much of favour to you."

When Panditji would never agree to stay back on any account, Sethji got disappointed and asked him, "then in what other way can I be of use to you? Please order. I could not listen to you to my satisfaction. If ever you come this way, please do show up."

Panditji – "If you are so keen, I shall definitely visit."

Saying this, Panditji stood up. Hesitation tied up his tongue once again. All this respect and concern are only because I am hiding my selfish motive. If he expressed his real intention, Sethji's tone might change. He may not get an empty response but definitely there will be no devotion. He got down to the street and stood thinking for a minute as to where will he go next. During winter, he used to freely go around on the expenditure of a spendthrift! When he himself was confused and was not ready to ask anybody, why would anybody give him anything? 'Does anybody know what's going on in my mind? Gone are the days when the wealthy people offered *pujas* to Brahmins! Give up the hope that some great man will come and offer you money on his own!' He walked slowly. Presently, Sethji called him out, "Panditji, please hold on."

Panditji stopped. He must be calling him to take him home. 'He has not parted with even a rupee yet and God knows what he wants to do taking me home!' But when Sethji placed a gold coin at his feet, Panditji was overwhelmed with gratitude and his eyes welled up. 'Even today, there are a few philanthropists on this planet, lest it be doomed to hell.' At that point Panditji was ready even to part with a *seer* or more than that of his blood for the welfare of this Sethji. In a delighted tone Panditji said, "this has no value for me Sethji. I am not a beggar but your servant."

Sethji said in a very humble and polite tone, "Lord, please accept this. This is not alm but my gift. I too can recognize people. Many saints, sanyasis, yogis and religious servants keep coming to me but I had never felt so devoted to anybody so far. I would only keep trying to somehow relieve myself from them. Observing your hesitation, I could easily say this is not your profession. You are an intellectual and pure-hearted, in some deep trouble. Please accept this meagre gift and bless me."

Panditji bought the medicines and went back with feelings of happiness, relief and victory at his heart. Lord Hanuman would have not felt this happy while flying back with the Sanjeevani herb (as per the legend the Lord Hanuman unable to identify the Sanjeevani herb on it, carried an entire hillock in a hurry, to save Lord Lakshmana)! He had never felt this kind of true happiness ever in his life. Never had his heart been filled with such pious feelings!

The day was sinking fast. The sun God was proceeding towards the West on a fast pace. Was he also in a hurry to save some sick persons? He quickly ran and hid himself behind the hills. Panditji walked briskly with longer strides as if he wanted to catch sun God. Darkness set in. A few stars started twinkling. He was yet to cross another ten miles. Just as a housewife runs around quickly to collect dry wigs when it gets cloudy, Leeladhar started running. He was not afraid of loneliness but was weary of losing his way in the darkness. He went past many *basthis to his left and right.*

This time Panditji felt it very comfortable in these villages. People were sitting around fire, relaxing and warming themselves up. Suddenly he· saw a dog, which came from nowhere and started leading Panditji in a fast stride. He was startled for a second but then he recognized the dog. He was the old man Choudhary's dog Mothi. Why did he come this far away from the village today? Was he aware that Panditji was arriving with the medicines and he may lose his way? God knows! When he called his name, he just wagged his tail but kept walking. Looked like he did not want to waste his time in further introduction. Panditji felt God was with him and he was protecting him. Now he was sure of reaching home safely. He reached home by ten in the night.

The disease was not fatal but fame was Panditji's slave! In a week all the three sick persons recovered. Panditji's fame reached far corners. He had fought a fierce battle with the Lord of death Yama and saved these persons. He had won over the Gods and made impossible possible. He himself was the God. People travelled from far and wide to have a look at him. But Panditji was not as pleased with his fame as he was on seeing the patients up on their feet.

Choudhary said, "Maharaj, you are the God. Had you not appeared, we would have not been saved."

Panditji- "I did nothing. All this is God's grace."

Choudhary-"Now we will never let you go. Go fetch your children too."

Panditji- "Even I am thinking alike. I cannot leave you and go."

Seeing the empty ground, they kept tight vigil on the nearby villages. Entire villages were getting converted to Islam. The Hindu Sabha remained unperturbed. Nobody had the guts to come down south. They were firing bullets at the Muslims from long distance. The biggest issue concerning them was the way in which they could avenge this murder. They kept appealing to the officials to investigate the matter in depth but they got the reply that the culprits were still at large. A fund was being created to build a memorial in

Panditji's name. But this new brightness was fading the colours of the Mullahs. Here was a new incarnation, who could make dead men alive and who was ready to sacrifice his life for the sake of his devotees. How could the Mullahs match this accomplishment, this dignity and this splendor? How can the cheap agents of heaven and Gods ever face such a splendid favour? Paditji was no more the Panditji who was proud of his Brahminism. He had learned to respect the Shudras and Bhils (considered lower castes). He never despised embracing them, anymore. They were leaning towards Islam only when their own houses were in dark. When the bright rays of the sun lit their houses, what was the need for them to go anywhere else? Sanathan Dharma (Hinduism) finally won. Incantations were heard in many villages and the sound of temple bells and conches were heard morning and evening. The behavior of the people bettered on its own. Panditji did not purify anybody. Panditji was ashamed to think that he had come to purify these people. 'How can I purify these people? Let me first purify myself. I cannot demean pure and holy souls in the name of purification.'

He learnt this *manthra* from these lower caste people and only on its strength he was successful in protecting his religion. Panditji is still alive and living along with his family in this state amongst the Bhils (a mountain tribe).

Kazhaki

This is an engaging tale of child psychology but since the end is tragic, it leaves us with a heavy heart. This is about the intimate friendship between a little boy and Kazhaki. Even slight carelessness may result in tragic situations.

Kazhaki is an unforgettable character in my childhood memories. It is forty years since; yet the figure of Kazhaki dances in my memory fresh. I used to live with my father in one of the regions of Azamgarh. Kazhaki was a *pasi* (a low caste, a hunter tribe*)*, a very lively, cheerful and brave character. Every evening he would bring the bag of letters, stay back in the night and go back with a bag of letters in the morning. In the evening, he would once again come back with a bag of letters.

I would be eagerly awaiting for him everyday. I would go out to the road restlessly and stand there. In a while, I would find Kazhaki running towards me with a bag on his shoulder and jingling anklet bells. He was a dark-skinned tall and sturdy young man. His physique was so well-proportioned that even an accomplished sculptor could not find any defect in it. His small mustache looked very nice on his graceful face. He would speeden up on seeing me and his anklet bells would ring faster just as my heart-beats. In extreme happiness I would run to him and in a moment his shoulder would become my throne. That was the heaven of my aspirations. Even the residents of heaven may not have experienced the kind of tumultuous happiness that I experienced on the broad shoulders of Kazhaki. The entire world seemed worthless at that moment and as Kazhaki ran around carrying me on his shoulders, I felt I was flying on a wind-horse!

When Kazhaki reached the post office he would be drenched in perspiration but he was not in the habit of resting. Immediately after handing over the letter bag, he would go along with us to some play ground and play games with us or entertain us with his songs or stories. He knew hundreds of stories of robbery, piracy, fights and ghosts. I would get engrossed with excitement and happiness in his stories. The robbers and plunderers of his stories were real warriors, who looted the rich and took care of the poor and helpless lives in distress. Instead of hatred, I would in fact respect them.

One day there was a delay in his getting the letter bag. He did not arrive until sun-set. I stood on the roadside and looked eagerly as far as my sight could reach but there was no sign of those familiar steps anywhere. My intent and sharp ears could not hear the delightful sound of those anklet bells. My hope started fading along with the daylight. Whenever someone came from that direction, I inquired, 'Is Kazhaki coming?' But some people just did not pay heed to my inquiry while some just shook their heads negatively. Suddenly, I heard the anklet bells. In darkness I would see only spirits in all directions and even the sweets on the shelf in my mother's room would seem trash to me, but the moment I heard the anklet bells I ran fast in that direction in the darkness. Yes, It was Kazhaki. The moment I saw him, my joy turned into anger. I beat him and stood angrily at a distance.

Kazhaki said smilingly, "If you beat me, I won't give you something which I have brought." With difficulty, I said, "Okay. Go! Don't give me. I won't even take it." Kazhaki – "If I show it now, you will immediately snatch it and embrace it." I melted and said, "Okay then. Go ahead and show it." Kazhaki - "Then first come and sit on my shoulder. Let me run. Today, I have come very late. Babuji might be angry." Without giving up I said, "First show that to me." I won. Had Kazhaki not been in a hurry and waited there even for another minute, things would have turned topsy turvy. He showed something which he held close to his chest. It had a long face and two sparkling eyes.

I ran to him and snatched it from his hands. It was a deer lamb. Ah! Who could guage the limit of my happiness at that moment?After that I passed very difficult examinations, attained top posts, even became a Rai Bahadur but never have I experienced that kind of happiness that I felt on that day. I started running towards my home, caressing the soft skin of the lamb on the way. I had no care as to why Kazhaki had come so late on that day.

I asked him, "Where did you find this Kazhaki?" Kazhaki- "Brother, just a little away from here there is a forest. There are many deer there. I was always hoping to find a lamb some day that I could bring for you. Today I spotted this lamb in a herd of deer. As I neared the herd, all of them started running. This lamb too started running but I did not give up my chase. All the deer ran very far away and only this lamb was left behind. I caught it. That's why I got delayed."

So chatting, we both reached the post office. Babuji neither saw me nor the deer lamb in my hands. He only saw Kazhaki. Angrily he said, "Why are you so late today? You have brought the bag at this hour. What should I do with it now? The postal van has already left. Tell me what caused this much of delay." Kazhaki stood dumbfounded.

Babuji said, "Maybe you don't need the job now. You are after all a low-caste fellow. Once you fed yourself, you have become fat. Only when you suffer hunger will you realise." Kazhaki stood silently. This enraged Babuji even more. He said, "Okay. Keep the bag down and find your way home. Swine! Has brought the post bag now. What do you lose? You can go and earn your wages anywhere. I will lose face and I will be questioned." Kazhaki said with welled up eyes, "In future I will never ever delay." Babuji- "Why this delay today? Answer me."

Kazhaki had no answer to this question. It was strange that even my tongue was tied. Babuji was very hot tempered. The very fact that he had to work would irritate him for every little thing. I never went anywhere near him. He too did not love me any time. He would come home twice a day for an hour each for his meals and spend all day in the office writing something. He kept appealing to the officials for an assistant but in vain. Even on holidays, Babuji was in his office. Only my mother knew to pacify him but how could she go to the office? Kazhaki was fired right in front of my eyes. His lance, turban and badge were snatched and he was ordered to leave the post office immediately. Ah! At that time I wished I had a bag of gold that I could give Kazhaki and show my father that by his firing Kazhaki, he could not harm even a single hair of Kazhaki. Kazhaki was as proud of his badge as a warrior would be of his spear. As he removed his badge, his hands shivered and his eyes filled with tears.

The root cause of all this problem, the delicate lamb was hiding its face in my hands and sitting comfortably like a child on a mother's lap. I followed Kazhaki slowly, as he started walking away from the post office. When we reached my home, he said, "brother, now you go home. It is night time." I stood silently struggling to control my tears. Kazhaki said, "brother, I would go out for some time and then return to carry you on my shoulders and play around. What if Babuji has fired me from my service, won't he let me do this? I will not leave you and go anywhere brother. Go tell your mother that Kazhaki is going away and she should pardon him for any misgivings."

I ran into the house but instead of telling anything to my mother, I started weeping uncontrollably. My mother came out of the kitchen and asked me, "what happened son? Who harmed you? Did Babuji say anything? Okay! Hold on. Let him come home and I shall question him. He always keeps hurting my son. Keep quiet son. You don't go to him any more."

With difficulty I controlled myself and told her, "Kazhaki…." My mother thought Kazhaki had beaten me and said, "Okay! Let Kazhaki come! I will get him fired immediately. How dare he beat my son! Right today I will get his badge and turban snatched away. Wah!". I quickly said, "No. Kazhaki did not beat me. Babuji fired him from service and took away his lance, turban and badge. Amma- "your babuji has committed a very grave mistake. That poor fellow is so honest in his work. Why did he fire him?" I said, "today he was late."

Saying this, I put the deer lamb down. At home I need not be afraid that he might run away. Till then my mother had not seen the lamb. Seeing it jump about, she got shocked and quickly held my hand, as though I would be bitten by that dangerous animal! Here I was weeping incessantly and suddenly on seeing my mother's fear, I started laughing heartily. Ammi – "Arre, this is a deer lamb. Where did you get this?" I narrated the entire history of the lamb uptill the tragic end of the story –"Amma, this was running so fast that nobody else could have caught it. It was flying off like wind. Kazhaki ran behind it for nearly five to six hours. Only then he could catch it. Ammaji, nobody in this world can run as fast as Kazhaki. Only because of this, he got delayed and only because of all this Babuji removed him from service and snatched away his turban, badge and lance. What will the poor fellow do now? He will die of hunger." Amma asked me, "Where is Kazhaki? Go fetch him for a while." I replied, "He is standing outside. He asked me to tell you to pardon him for any of his misdeeds."

Uptil then my mother thought my story was imaginary. Maybe she thought Babuji might have just scolded Kazhaki. After listening to my last sentence, she got the suspicion that Kazhaki might have been fired in reality. She went out of the house and called out, "Kazhaki, Kazhaki…." But there was no sign of Kazhaki. I too called him out many times but he was not there. I did have my dinner. Afterall kids do not forgo meals, especially when a delicious dish like *rabdi* (a sweet dish made out of milk cream) was laid before them! But I lay on my bed thinking till late night, 'if I had money, I would have given Kazhaki a lakh of rupees and tell him, 'don't ever talk to Babuji.' Poor man will die of hunger. Let me see whether he comes tomorrow or not. What would he do coming here? But he said he would come. From tomorrow, I will feed him when I have my meals.' I kept building such castles in the air and fell asleep. On the following day, I spent all my time taking care of my deer lamb.

First of all I conducted the naming ceremony of the lamb. I named it 'Munnoo.' Then I introduced him to all my classmates and friends. Just in a day, he got so attached to me that he ran behind me wherever I went. Within a short time, I gave him a very important place in my life. I had even decided to allocate a separate room in the palatial house that I was going to build in my future life. I even planned on a mat and a phaeton (a four-wheeled carriage) to take him around.

But in the evening, I kept aside all these thoughts and stood by the road, looking for Kazhaki. I knew Kazhaki had been dismissed and it was not necessary for him to come here anymore. Even then I had a hope that he would definitely come. Suddenly I had a flash that Kazhaki might be dying of hunger. I immediately went into my home. Amma was lighting the lamp. I stealthily took some flour in a basket, holding on to the flour in my hand and ran out dropping the flour all along the route. I just went to the roadside when I saw Khazaki coming. He had the turban on, wore the badge and carried the lance too. The letter bag too was tied on his back. I ran and hugged him from his back and said with a surlprise, "Where did you get your badge and turban Kazhaki?" Kazhaki carried me and made me sit on his shoulder. He said, "Of what use was that badge brother? That was a badge of slavery but this badge is of good memories. Earlier I was a Government servant but now I am your servant." So saying, he spotted the basket.

He said, "what is this flour for brother?" I hesitatingly said, "I brought it only for you. You might be hungry. What would you have eaten today?" I could not see Kazhaki's eyes, as I was sitting on his shoulder but I could definitely make out from his voice that his throat was choking. He said, "brother, can I eat just dry *rotis*?" "But how can I bring salt, ghee and dal. Now my ammi would be alert. I somehow ran out with this flour. (I had not realized even then that my theft had already been revealed and the white line that I had dropped all along my way was the clue). How can I bring three things out? If I ask ammi, she will never give. She makes me cry for hours to part with just a single paisa; how would she part with three things?" Suddenly I remembered that I had kept a few coins and notes in between my cloth bag meant for books. I took pleasure in saving money. I wonder why I gave up that habit. Had I been of the same nature, maybe I would not have been so helpless now. Babuji never ever loved me but he would give me a lot of money, maybe he found that the easiest way to keep me away from his office. He was afraid of my tantrums in case he refused. He controlled this nonsense from a distance. My mother's nature was quite opposite to this. My tantrums in no way disturbed any of her activities. Someone can put up with the noise of crying all day while just lying down but if he is accounting, the noise really disturbs his concentration. Ammi loved me a lot but her temper changed immediately on the mention of money. I did not have books but I did have a bag in which I had a notebook stitched out of some postal forms. I wondered whether the few coins that I had saved would be enough to buy dal, salt and ghee. I had a handful of coins after all. I decided and said, "Okay, let me down. I will go fetch ghee, dal and salt but will you come everyday?"

Kazhaki, "brother, why will I not come if you feed me everyday?" I said, "I will bring you food everyday." Kazhaki said, "then I will come everyday." I got down and came running with all my savings. To ensure that Kazhaki came everyday, I was ready even to hand over the precious Kohinoor diamond, if I had it. Kazhaki was taken aback and asked, "where did you get this money from brother?" I answered proudly, "it is my money." Kazhaki- "your ammi will beat you. She will say Kazhaki snatched this money from you cunningly. Buy some sweets with this money and save them in a pot. I will not die hungry. I have two hands. Why would I die of hunger?"

However much I convinced Kazhaki that the money was my own, he refused to accept it. He took me around the village for a long time, singing songs for me on the way, dropped me back at home and left. He placed the basket with flour at my doorsteps. The moment I stepped into my house, my mother reprimanded me, "Thief! Where did you take the flour? You are now learning to rob? Tell me, to whom did you give the flour! Or else I will beat you blue and black." I was trapped.My mother would turn into a lioness when she was angry. I was in a fix and blabbered, "I did not give anybody." Amma-"did you not take out the flour? Look how much of flour is fallen all over the courtyard." I stood dumb. Her threat or coaxes did not move me. My tongue was drying up with fear of the upcoming disaster. I was so tongue-tied that it did not even occur to me to tell her, "why are you getting upset? The flour is right at the doorstep". Neither could I go fetch the flour. It seemed I had become totally inactive and my legs had lost all strength to move. Just then, Kazhaki called out, "Bahuji, the flour is at the doorstep. The lad had brought the flour to give me."

My mother went towards the door once she heard this. She never followed purda system with Kazhaki. I do not know whether she spoke anything to Kazhaki but I saw her come back with the empty basket. She went into the room, took something out of the trunk and went to the door. I saw her closed fist. I could no longer stand there. I followed my mother. Amma called out from the doorway many times but Kazhaki had already gone away. I impatiently asked her, "Shall I go and look for him Ammaji?" Ammaji latched the door and said, "where will you go in this darkness. Just a while ago, he was right here. I had told him to wait here and I would be back in a minute. I wonder where he escaped so soon. He is a very shy person. He hesitated so much to accept the flour. I forcefully poured it in his *angochi* (A piece of cloth worn around the shoulders) and tied it. I feel very sorry for the poor guy. I wonder whether the poor chap has something to eat in his house. I had brought some money to give him but I don't know where he went away." Now I too got some courage. I narrated the entire story of my theft. Parents cannot influence their children's learning as elders, as much as they can, by becoming understanding children among their children. Ammaji said, "why didn't you ask me? Would I have not given a little flour for Kazhaki?"

I did not answer this question. I said to myself, 'at present you feel compassionate about Kazhazi. That's why you are ready to give whatever you please. But had I demanded, you would have beaten me up.' Of course, I felt relieved that Kazhaki would definitely not go hungry now. Ammiji will give something to Kazhaki everyday and he will tour me around on his shoulders every day. On the next day, I played with Munnoo all day long. In the evening, I went and stood by the road. Darkness set in but there was no sign of Kazhaki. The lamps were lit and eerie silence spread all over but Kazhaki did not turn up. I came home crying. Ammaji asked me, "why are you crying my son? Did Kazhaki not turn up?" I started crying louder. Ammaji hugged me. I could feel she was also getting choked up. She said, "son, stop crying. Tomorrow I will send words through somebody and beckon Kazhaki." I went off to sleep, as I wept incessantly. The moment I opened my eyes in the morning, I told my mother, "Fetch Kazhaki." Ammi said, "Someone has gone to get him son. Kazhaki might be on his way." I started playing happily. I knew that Ammaji would always keep up her word. She had sent a messenger early in the morning. Around ten in the morning, when I returned with Munnoo, I came to know that Kazhaki was not found in his house. In fact, he had not even returned home the previous night. His wife was grief-stricken and worried about his whereabouts. She feared that he must have fled away somewhere. Nobody can guage how sensitive kids are. Kids will have no words to express their feelings. They cannot even say what cripples their minds, what pricks their hearts, why they feel like weeping, why they sit back morosely and they do not find any interest in playing. I was in such a state. I kept running in and out of the house and standing by the road now and then. My eyes were searching for Kazhaki. 'Where has he gone away? Hope he has not run away!' I stood with a lost look by the road during late evening. Just then I saw Kazhaki on one of the lanes. Yes. That was Kazhaki. I ran towards him, calling him out but on reaching the lane, there was no sign of Kazhaki. Where had he vanished?

I searched from one end of the lane to the other end but could find no trace of Kazhaki. I went home and told my mother about this. I realized Ammaji got very worried about the whole thing. Kazhaki did not show up for two to three days after that. I had even started slowly forgetting him. Kids can become as cold-hearted as they can love. They can destroy the same toy that they loved a lot just 3-4 days before. Another 10-12 days passed by. It was afternoon and Babuji was having his lunch. I was tying anklets to the legs of Munnoo. One woman stood at our door step, removing her veil. Her clothes were dirty and tattered but she was fair and pretty.

She asked me, "brother, where is bahuji?" I went near her, looked at her face and asked her, "who are you? What do you sell?" The woman- "I don't sell anything. I have brought some *kamalgatte* (the seeds of lotus) for you. You love these sweets, don't you brother?" I looked at the packet in her hand with excitement and asked her, "Where have you brought them from? Let me see!" The woman – "Your messenger has sent them for you brother." I jumped up and asked, "Kazhaki?" The woman shook her head and answered, "yes" and started opening the packet. By then Ammiji came out of the kitchen. The woman touched my mother's feet. Amma asked her, "Are you Kazhaki's wife?" The woman bent down her head. Amma- "what does Kazhaki do these days?" The woman started crying and replied, "Bahuji, from the day he brought flour from you, he has fallen ill. He keeps chanting 'brother, brother'. His heart is with brother. Suddenly he wakes up with a start and runs to the door calling out 'brother'. I don't know what has become of him Bahuji. One day he ventured out without telling me, hid himself in a lane and kept looking at brother. But when brother spotted him, he ran away from there. He feels shy to come to you." I said, "Ammiji, didn't I tell you the other day?" Amma- "Do you have something to eat, at home?" The woman- "yes Bahuji! With your blessings, we have enough to feed ourselves. Today morning he woke up and went towards the lake. I begged him not to go out lest he get a fever but he did not listen to me. His legs were shivering out of weakness but he got into the lake and brought these lotus seeds out. Then he told me, 'go take these seeds for my brother. He loves them. Find out about his welfare.'" I had already started happily chewing the seeds from the packet. Amma tried to signal me to control myself but in vain. Amma said, "tell him everything is fine here." I said, "also tell him his brother is calling him and he would not talk to him if he does not turn up". Babuji finished his lunch and came out. Drying his hand with a towel, he said, "also tell him that Saheb has reinstated him and if he does not come immediately, somebody else will be appointed. The woman covered her head with the veil once again and went away. Ammaji called her back many times, but she did not stop. Maybe Ammaji wanted to give her the information herself. She asked Babuji, "he has really been reinstated?" Babuji, "what else? Am I calling him to fool? I had issued the reinstatement orders on the fifth day itself." Amma – "you have done a good thing". Babuji – "this is the medicine for his illness."

What do I see as soon as I woke up the next morning? Kazhaki was coming, propping his *lathi.*He had become very weak and his old age was showing up. A green tree had dried up and become barren. I ran to him and hugged his waist. Kazhaki kissed my cheek and attempted to carry me on his shoulders but I could not get on to him. He then fell on his four limbs like an animal and I sat on his back. He started crawling towards the post office with me. There was no limit for my happiness at that moment and maybe Kazhaki too was very happy. Babuji said, "Kazhaki, you are reappointed. Do not come late in future." Kazhaki fell at Babuji's feet with tears in his eyes. But maybe I was not fated to enjoy both the pleasures at the same time. When I found Munnoo, Kazhaki was gone and now when Kazhaki returned Munnoo had escaped from me. The sorrow of losing him haunts me till date. Munnoo used to eat from my plate. He would not touch the food until I sat along to eat. He loved rice a lot but would never relish it until enough ghee was not added to it. He would sleep along with me and wake up when I woke up. He loved cleanliness and would run out to the open field to answer nature's calls. He hated dogs and would never let them enter the house. The moment he spotted a dog, he would stop eating and run to drive the dog out. When I dropped Kazhaki at the post office and went home to eat, Munnoo too joined me. We had eaten just a few morsels, when we spotted a furry dog in our quadrangle. Munnoo started running the moment he saw the dog. A dog becomes a rat when in an alien house. The dog started running seeing Munnoo sprinting towards him. It was time for Munnoo to return but the dog turned out to be the God of his death. Munnoo was not satisfied with driving away the dog out of the quadrangle. He started chasing him even on the field outside. Probably Munnoo did not realise that he was outside his jurisdiction. He reached an area, where dogs too had the same rights as Munnoo. Maybe Munnoo had become very proud of his great strength, driving dogs. He did not understand that at home, he had the support of his master. The moment he entered that field, the dog bit his neck and poor Munnoo could not even shout. I heard the shouts of my neighbours and ran out but Munnoo lay dead and there was no sign of the furry dog.

Babaji's Feast

Sometimes superstition results in problems and adversities for us. The poor farmer would borrow foodgrains, flour and ghee to feed the sadhus and saints who came to his doorsteps. The sadhus would go fully satisfied, while the family was left hungry!

A sadhu stood at the door of Ramdhan Ahir and said, "son, may you be blessed! Please show respect to this sadhu". Ramdhan told his wife, "A sadhu has arrived. Go give him something."

Wife – "I was washing the vessels and deeply engrossed in the worry as to what I would cook for lunch today, as there is not a grain at home." It was the month of Chaitha (the beginning of summer) but darkness set in right from afternoon in that house. The grannery was empty. Half the yield was taken away by the money-lender while the other half was taken away by the Zamindar's tax collectors. They escaped from the clutches of the trader who sold them his bullocks, by selling the husk. They were just left with just a few bundles of grains as their share. They could extract just about a *mann (*40 *seers*) of grain by pounding that. Somehow, the month of Chaith passed by. What next? What will the bullocks eat and what will the family members feed on – God in heaven knows. But a sadhu has arrived at the doorstep. How to send him disappointed? What will he think?

Wife – "what shall I give? There is nothing left."

Ramdhan – "Go check in the mud pot. If you find some left over flour, get that."

Wife – "Yesterday I cooked whatever I could scrouge out of the pot, by washing it clean. Will the pot produce something out of nothing?"

Ramdhan – "I cannot go and tell the sadhu that there is nothing at home. Go borrow something from somebody else's house."

Wife – "I am yet to return what I have already borrowed from people. What face have I got to go and beg for more?"

Ramdhan – "Have we not reserved some portion for the God? Fetch that."

Wife – "Then how do we worship the Gods?"

Ramdhan – "Gods don't come and demand. If possible we shall worship, if not we may not."

Wife – "Arre! Even that may be just a few handfuls, maybe just about half *a seer*. Is this the last sadhu to visit us? We have to cut a sorry figure at least in front of the next sadhu!"

Ramdhan – "at least we will pass through this time. Let's handle future occasions when the time comes."

The lady went in murmering to herself and brought out a small vessel containing about half a *seer*of flour. That was saved with a lot of difficulty for the sake of the Gods. Ramdan held it in his hand and stood thoughtfully for a few seconds. Then he went out and dropped the flour in the sadhu's bag.

The sadhu accepted the flour and said, "my son, now this sadhu shall stay put here today. If you just give me some dal, sadhu's meal will be complete." Ramdhan went in and told his wife about the sadhu's plan. Incidentally, there was a little dal at home. Ramdhan handed over the dal, salt and dried cow dung cakes to the sadhu. Then he drew some water from the well for the sadhu. The sadhu very ceremoniously cooked the dal, made rotis and also some curry out of the potato that he had in his bag. When everything was ready, the sadhu told Ramdhan, "To offer this feast to the God, I need a spoonful of ghee. If the food is not sanctified with ghee, how can I offer it to the God?"

Ramdhan – "Babaji, there is no ghee at home."

Sadhu – "You have a lot of blessings from the God. Don't say such things."

Ramdhan – "Maharaj, I do not have a cow or a buffalo. Wherefrom should I get ghee?"

Sadhu – "There is everything in the Almighty's store."

Ramdhan went in and told his wife, "he is asking for ghee. After all he is begging for alms and he cannot digest the food without ghee!"

Wife – "Okay! Take some dal from the left over portion to the *baniya* (grocer) and get some ghee in exchange. When we have managed to give him so much, why earn his ire just for a spoon of ghee?" Thus the ghee arrived! Sadhuji removed the metal gong from his bag and beat it with a ball of thread, as he got ready to make the offering to the God. He relished the food and ate it all up. Then he carassed his stomach with his hand and lay down near the door. Ramdhan took the vessels, plate and ladles for washing, into the house.

That night, Ramdhan's family members had to make do with just a bit of cooked dal.

Ramdhan thought, as he lay on his bed, 'this sadhu is much better than me.'

The Grain-Pounder's Well

This story describes how greed compels man to forget his promises and how selfishness becomes a coquetry, in a very interesting manner. She fulfils her dream of making a well in memory of her husband only on her death!

Gomathi lay on her death bed. She told Choudhary Vinayak Singh, "Choudhary, this was my life's aspiration."

Choudhary seriously replied, "Do not worry about that Kaaki. God will fulfil your desire. I will get people to work on it right from today. God willing, you shall drink the water from your well. You should have counted. How much money do you have?"

Gomathi closed her eyes for a moment and recollected with difficulty, "Bhaiyya, how do I know how much I have? Whatever I have is in this container. Ensure that the work is completed with this much money. Whom can we borrow money from?"

Choudhary weighed the closed container with his hands and said, "we have to manage only with this Kaaki. Who will lend money? Not a bit of alm comes out of any house; so who will give money to dig a well? Blessed are you, who have saved all your lifetime earnings for this noble cause!"

Gomathi proudly said, "Bhaiyya, you were very young then. When your Kaaka died, I did not have a penny on me. I used to starve for days. Whatever he had was all spent on his medical treatment. He was a great devotee of God. That's why God took him away so soon. Since then you have seen how I am struggling to lead my life. I had huge quantities of grain on many nights and people used to be astonished. I don't know from where I would get all that strength. My only desire was to dig a small well in my husband's memory in this village. The legacy has to continue. Only for this reason man yearns to have children."

Thus she left her will with Choudhary Vinayak Singh and breathed her last that night. The last words that emerged from her mouth before Gomathi died were, "do not delay getting the well dug." People doubted that she had any wealth but were sure she had two thousand rupees. The old woman used to hide her savings very safely. Choudhary was the village chief and he was a very honest man. That is why the old woman gave this final order of hers to him.

Choudhary did not spend much on Gomathi's last rites. The moment he completed the rites, he requested his son Harnath Singh to get an estimate of the bricks, mortor and stones required for the well. Harnath was dealing in grocery. He listened to his father silently for some time and then said, "will it matter anything if there is a delay of another few months in making the well?"

Choudhary said, "Yes. Of course there is no great harm in a delay of a few months but what is the reason to delay? She has already given the money; we shall earn fame free of cost! Gomathi has asked me to make the well soon, in her dying statement."

Harnath – "Yes. She did say so. But the market is doing well these days. If we hoard foodgrains worth two-three thousand rupees, we can earn a good profit in the months of *margasheesh* and *pushya.* I will give you some interest." Choudhary was filled with fear and confusion. 'what if the two thousands becomes two and a half thousands? Maybe I could buy some asset. But what if there is a reduction in the fund?'

He could not hide his fear and said, "what if there is a loss?"

Harnath hesitatingly replied, "is there any reason for making a loss?"

"Imagine, if there is a loss, then what?"

Harnath replied with irritation, "say this that you do not want to part with the money. Aren't you a great saint?"

Choudhary too was submissive to his son like any other old man. He replied in a worried tone, "When did I tell you that I will not give you the money? But this is somebody else's money and we have to think twice before we use it. Who can predict about commerce and business? What if the prices fall further? The grains can get spoilt due to some disease or get destroyed in a fire. Think well of all eventualities."

Harnath sarcastically said, "if you are so pessimistic, why not think that some thief could steal the entire fund or the well could collapse immediately after construction? Even such things can happen!"

Choudhary could not argue any further. The weak soldier claps his hands and enters the warfield but once he faces a shining sword, he starts shivering. Switching sides instantly, Choudhary asked, "so, how much do you want?"

Harnath, like a safe warrior facing a retreating enemy, confidently replied, "give the entire sum. Do I want to play with small sums like fifty or hundred?"

Choudhary agreed. Nobody had seen Gomathi handing him over the money. There was no chance of people criticizing him. Harnath hoarded foodgrains. Sacks of grains were heaped up. Choudhary who used to sleep peacefully until then, now could not sleep well. He kept vigil of the stock of foodgrains, lest some mice enter the grannery. Choudhary so efficiently caught mice that even the cats would accept defeat! Six months passed by this way. By the month of *Pushya*the entire stock was sold and they earned a neat profit of five hundred rupees.

Harnath said, "you retain fifty rupees out of this."

Choudhary was shocked and said, "fifty rupees? Is this charity? If you had borrowed this sum from a money-lender, you would have paid a minimum of two hundred rupees as interest. Okay pay me a few rupees less, what else?"

Harnath did not prolong the conversation. He paid 150 rupees to Choudhary. Choudhary had never felt so happy in his life. When he went into his room to sleep, he felt like the old woman Gomathi was standing there and smiling at him. Choudhary's heart started beating louder. He was not sleeping. He was not intoxicated too. Gomathi was standing in front of him with a smile. Yes. There was a very strange nimbleness on that wrinkled face.

Many years passed by. Choudhary was always meaning to collect the entire money from Harnath but he kept dilly-dallying. He paid a little interest every year but found some pretext or the other to return the principal. Sometimes the excuse of some purchases and sometimes repaying some other debt. The business kept growing. In the end on one day Choudhary very clearly said, "I don't care whether your business runs or fails, you have to definitely return the sum this month." Harnath gave many lame excuses but Choudhary was firm in his decision.

Harnath said with irritation, "I am asking to wait for two more months. Once the stock is sold, I will repay you."

Choudhary firmly said, "your stock will never be sold and your two-month time will never come. I will get my money today."

Harnath got up angrily at that moment, brought out two thousand rupees and threw it with force at his father.

Choudhary said with a shock, "so, you did have the money."

"Then do you think life runs just on words?"

"Okay. Give me five hundred rupees now and the balance after two months. The entire money will not be spent in one day."

Harnath said with disgust, "you may spend the money or deposit it. I have nothing to do with it anymore. Are all the money-lenders of the town dead that I should bear your taunts?"

Choudhary took the money and kept it on a shelf. All his enthusiasm of drawing up a plan for the well died down.

Harnath returned the money well, but had some ulterior motive in his mind. At midnight, when there was silence all over, he opened Choudhary's room door and entered it. Choudhary was fast asleep. Harnath actually wanted to take away both the bags and go out but just as he extended his hand towards the bags, he saw Gomathi standing there. She was holding both the bags in her two hands. Harnath retreated with a start.

Then he thought he must have been deceived by his imagination and once again extended his hand towards the bags but this time the image became all the more horrifying. He could not stand there even for a moment. He ran out but fell swoon in the verandah.

Harnath had collected his dues from various people and saved the same to pay up his creditors. When Choudhary lost his temper, Harnath had threw the same money at him. He had made up his mind at that very moment that he would take the money away at night and raise a false alarm of some intruder, which would not put him under suspicion. But as this plan of his failed, he started getting pressurized by his creditors. He did his best to buy time on his words and gave all possible excuses that he could think of. In the end, people threatened to sue him. One of them went to the extent of suing him for three hundred rupees. Poor Choudhary was in great difficulty. Harnath was managing the business and Choudhary had no connection with it. Yet people trusted him only because they trusted Choudhary, who was a very straight-forward and honest person. Even now, nobody was blaming Choudhary but he was escaping from people's gaze. But he had decided that he would not touch the money meant for the well, come what may. One night, a Muslim servant of a trader came to his doorstep and rained a thousand abuses on him. Choudhary got enraged many times and felt like exhibiting his ire, but his mind convinced him that in no way he was concerned; nor was he obliged to repay the debts of the son.

When he went for his meals, his wife said, "what's all this commotion about?"

Choudhary shot back with irritation, "Have I caused all this confusion?"

"Who else is the cause? Our son says he has very little money and you have taken away most of it."

Choudhary – "I had no other way but to demand that money from him; I don't like mixing up issues like going to the sweet shop and eating sweets myself and claiming that I am actually eating on my dead grandfather's behalf, who shall actually get the reward (this is a proverb in Hindi reading *halwai ki dukan par dada ka fatheha padna)*."

Wife – "You enjoy this snobbery?"

Choudhary – "Is it under my control? Will I ever make a well or not? Already five years have passed by."

Wife – "He has not eaten anything now. He was just about to put the first morsel into his mouth but he left."

Choudhary – "You did not make him understand the situation and feed him properly. He won't get the money by sacrificing his meal."

Wife – "Why don't you go and convince him?"

Choudhary – "He will now see me as an enemy."

Wife – "I will go hand over the money to Harnath. When we get that kind of money again, the well may be dug."

Choudhary – "No. Don't you ever do such a thing! I cannot commit such a deceitful act in my life, even if my house crumbles down."

But his wife did not pay attention to these words. She instantly went into the room and was just about to lay her hands on the bags but moved away with a scream. Her entire body was shivering like the strings of a sitar.

Choudhary got scared and asked her, "What happened? I hope you are not giddy!"

His wife looked towards the shelf with frightful eyes and said, "The witch is standing there."

Choudhary looked in the same direction and asked, "Which witch? I don't see anything there."

Wife – "My heart is beating so loud. I felt as though the old woman had caught hold of my hand."

Choudhary – "This is hallucination. The old woman died five years ago. Will she be sitting here until now?"

Wife – "I saw very clearly. It was the old woman. Even our son said he had seen her holding on to the bags in the night."

Choudhary – "When did he come into my room in the night?"

Wife – "He came into your room to say something about the money to you but ran out seeing the old woman there."

Choudhary – "Okay. Then go in. I shall watch."

His wife closed her ears and said, "No, no baba! I will never ever step into that room."

Choudhary – "Okay, then I shall go and check."

Choudhary went into the room and took both the bags. Nothing untoward happened. There was no sign of Gomathi's image anywhere. His wife was peeping into the room from the doorstep. Choudhary came out proudly and said, "I could not see anything there. If she was standing over there, where did she vanish?"

Wife – "How do I know why she does not appear to you? She was friendly with you. Maybe because of that, she vanished."

Choudhary – "You are hallicunating. Nothing else."

Wife – "I will call Harnath and ask him."

Choudhary – "I am right here. Why don't you come and check out?"

The wife felt reassured. She went to the shelf and extended her hand with fear; but she screamed loudly, ran out breathlessly to the quadrangle. Choudhary too ran to the quadrangle and asked her with astonishment, "What happened? You ran out for no reason. I could see nothing there." The woman's voice was shivering. She said with disgust, "Just move out, you had almost killed me. I don't know what'swrong with your eyes. The witch was right there."

Just then Harnath came there. Seeing his mother standing in the courtyard, he asked, "what's it Amma? How are you?"

Amma- "That witch showed up twice today my son! I thought I would hand over the money to you and get the well made when we get money. But just when I was about to lay my hands on the bags, the witch caught hold of my hands. I was almost dead with fear."

Harnath said, "We have to get some good sorcerer to drive this spirit away."

Choudhary – "Did you also see her in the night?"

Harnath – "Yes. I came to consult you regarding some issue. As soon as I stepped into your room, I found the witch standing near the shelf and ran out totally shocked."

Choudhary – "Okay, then go into the room now."

Wife – "Who? No way! I will not let anybody go in even if someone is ready to give me a lakh of rupees."

Harnath – "I will not go."

Choudhary – "But I don't see any spirit. Why so?"

Harnath – "How do I know? Maybe she is afraid of you. We have to call some sorcerer today."

Choudhary – "I am unable to understand what the matter is. What happened to Baiju Pandey's decree?"

Harnath was so angry with his father that he had stopped discussing any matter regarding his business, with him. He turned his face towards the courtyard and spoke, as though he was talking to the wind, "whatever has to happen will happen! Beyond taking away my life, what harm can anybody do to me? I cannot throw up whatever I have eaten up!"

Choudhary – "what if his decree is executed?"

Harnath – "So what? I have a stock worth about five to six hundred rupees. That will get attached."

Choudhary – "The entire business will go do dogs."

Harnath – "How long shall I cry over my failing business? If had known earlier that there was such an urgency in getting the well made, why would I have provoked the spirit? We were getting enough to feed ourselves. Under extreme circumstances, I may have to spend a few months in jail. What worse can happen?"

Amma – "I shall burn down the face of the one who dares to jail you! How can you be jailed when we are still alive?"

Harnath philosophically said, "Parents can be our companions in life and not in our fate!"

Choudhary had excessive love for his son. He started suspecting his son of planning to gobble away the money and hence he had hurriedly collected the money from him. He now realized that his son was really in trouble. He thought his family image would get blotted if his son goes to jail or his shop is attached. 'What's wrong if I use Gomathi's money to save him? After all, the business will continue and sometime or the other that money could be retrieved!'

All of a sudden someone from outside called out, "Harnath Singh!" Harnath turned pale. Choudhary inquired, "Who's that?"

"Attachment Officer (Amin)."

"What? Has he come to confiscate the shop?"

"Yes. It seems so."

"What is the value of the decree?"

"1500 rupees."

"Will the Amin not delay the proceedings if we tip him a bit?"

"He may agree to delay but the money-lender will also be with him. Whatever tip he expected, he would have collected from him."

"No, no. Give 1500 rupees out of Gomathi's funds."

"Who will touch her money? Nobody knows what calamity will strike our house by doing so!"

"Who is going to eat away her money? Come, let me only give the money."

Choudhary now got a fear lest she may appear to him also! But his suspicion failed. He removed 550 rupees from one bag, put it in the other bag and handed it over to Harnath. By evening, not a rupee was left out of the two thousand rupees!

Twelve years went by. Neither Choudhary nor Harnath is alive today. As long as he was alive, Choudhary worried about the well and kept meditating about it until his last breath. But there was always a shortage of funds in the shop. Immediately after Choudhary's death, there was a downfall in the business. Harnath was not content with the meagre profits made by him and aimed at doubling and tribbling his profits. He started gambling. Within a year the shop had to be shut.

Jewellry and all household assets were gone in no time. Exactly a year after Choudhary's death, Harnath too bid goodbye to this materialistic world. The women had no companion in this world. The senior woman fell ill but had no money to treat herself. She too suffered in many ways for 3-4 months and left the mortal world. Now Choudhary's daughter-in-law was left all alone and she was pregnant. She had nobody to support her. She could also not labour because of her physical condition. She somehow managed to lead her life by tailoring for the neighbours, for about six months. She thought all the signs indicated that she will beget a son and lived in the hope that she will get a life companion. But she delivered a daughter and lost even that hope. She became so disappointed and hardened, that she did not even hug her new born daughter. After the neighbours pacified her, she took the child in her hands but she had no milk to feed the child. Suddenly, there was an outburst of compassion, love and attachment in the mother's heart. She thought she would feel blessed if her barren breast somehow yielded even one drop of milk! On seeing the innocence, helpless and begging look, thirst and lustre of the child, it seemed like her motherly heart was being churned by thousands of eyes! All her good wishes, all her blessings, all her glory and all her love flowed out of her heart through her eyes on to the little child and entertained her in such a way as the cool radiance of the moonlight entertains a flower. But the comfort of mother's love was not fated for that unfortunate child! The mother fed a little of her milk, along with other feeds and brought her up but her own condition was deteriorating day after day.

One day people who visited her, found her fallen on the ground and the child sucking her breast. Where was the blood in that weak body battered by poverty and despair, to flow as milk? That child grew up on the charity and alms of the neighbours. One day the young girl went around cutting grass and reached the spot where Gomathi used to live. The roof was fully gone. Just a few broken walls remained. In places half-walls stood. For some strange reason, the girl started digging the earth with her sickle. She spent all afternoon doing this, unmindful of eating or drinking anything. She had no fear or suspicion. The sun set and darkness engulfed but she continued digging. Those days the farmers would never tread that way even by oversight! But the girl sat without any fear, digging the earth deeper and deeper. When it grew darker, she left.

On the next day, she woke up early and cut a lot of grass, more than she would have cut in a whole day, within no time. In the afternoon, she took her bag and sickle and reached the same spot that she had dug a hole the previous day. But today she was not alone but had another two boys with her. All the three of them kept digging the same spot until late evening. The girl kept digging, while the boys removed the soil so dug from the hole.

On the third day, another two boys joined the game. The game went on till evening. The hole was now as deep as the length of two arms. A very rare kind of excitement filled the hearts of the children of the village, playing this special game. On the fourth day, a few more kids joined. They discussed as to who would go in and dig, who would remove the soil and who would draw it out. The hole was now as deep as the length of four arms but except the children working there, no villager was aware of this. One night, a farmer reached that ruin, looking for his lost buffalo. He saw a heap of soil, a deep hole and a blinking lamp inside the ruin and ran out with fear. Many others went and checked. There were many of them. So fearlessly, they went closer and checked and found the girl sitting there. One man asked her, "Arre, is that you who dug this hole?"

The girl – "Yes."

"What for are you digging this?"

"I will make a well here."

"How can you make a well?"

"Just as I have dug this much, I will dig deeper. All the children of the village come here to help me in this game."

"Looks like you will die and will take with you all the other children too. Beware! Don't you dare continue digging here from tomorrow!"

On the following day, no kid turned up there and the girl too was busy with her work throughout the day. But in the evening, there was a lamp lit there and the girl was seen there with her sickle.

The villagers admonished her, even beat her up and kept her locked in a room. But she fled to that spot, if she ever got a chance. Villagers are after all devotional and seeing the little girl's unworldly passion, love bloomed in their hearts too. Thus they involved themselves in digging a well. As the elders kept digging the well, the girl started making bricks out of the soil removed from there. All the children of the village joined this game. Even when the entire village went off to sleep, she was seen making the bricks. God knows from where she got that kind of dedication. After all she was just seven years old! But in such a young age, she could challenge people thrice her age with her sharp tongue and intellect. Finally the well was ready and its frame walls were also built. On that day, the girl slept on that platform. Her happiness knew no bounds. She was laughing and singing.

Early in the morning, only her mortal remains were found on that platform surrounding the well. Since that day, the villagers say that the girl was none other than Gomathi herself. The well was named 'the grain-pounder's well'.

Atonement

When there is a gap in status on account of the posts held by two friends and they feel a kind of inequality, there may occasionally arise imaginary situations that result in tragic ends. When the glaring realitydawns, we are pushed to atone!

It is the style of officials to return late from offices. The higher the post, the more this habit of coming to the office very early and going home late. A peon is meant to be present all the 24 hours. He cannot even go on leave. He has to arrange for a substitute. Thus, when the Head Clerk Babu Madaarilal of Bareilly Zilla Board came to the office at eleven in the morning, it seemed like the entire office woke up from deep slumber. The peon ran to take his bicycle, the orderly ran to the cabin and raised the blinds and the *jamadar* quickly placed the folder of letters on the table. The moment Madaarilal opened the first Government order, his face turned pale. He stood transfixed for a few moments, as though all his sensory organs had gone numb. He had faced greater adversities but never had he been so shocked. The matter was that the Board had appointed Subodh Chandra to the post of Board Secretary, which was lying vacant for the previous one month. Madaarilal despised the very name of Subodh Chandra. Subodh Chandra was his classmate, whom he desired to overtake and put in his best efforts in that direction but always failed. The same Subodh was today coming as his senior officer. There was no news about Subodh in that town since long. He just knew that he had entered the armed forces. Madaarilal thought he must have died in action but today he has resurfaced and is coming here as his officer. Madaarilal will have to work under him. It was better to die than bear such an insult. Subodh will definitely remember all about the school and college days. Madaarilal had tried many times to get Subodh rusticated out of the college by making false allegations, conspiring against him and defaming him. Would Subodh have forgotten all that? Never! The moment he comes, he will avenge for all his past. Madaari Babu could not think of any idea to protect himself.

It seemed like the two were fated to be enemies by birth! Both of them joined the same school on the same day and on the very first day the spark of jealousy and hatred was lit in their hearts and that has never been extinguished until today, even after twenty years! The only sin of Subodh was that he beat Madaarilal in everything – physique, complexion, behavior, knowledge, studies and everything. Madaarilal never pardoned him for this sin, and he had ever remained like a thorn in his mind all these twenty years. When Subodh obtained his degree and went home and Madaarilal failed in his degree exams and landed in this job, only then he felt peaceful. When he heard that Subodh was going away to Basare, he felt delighted. The nagging noose was loosened from his heart. But how unfortunate! Today that old ulcer once again surfaced in his heart and it was hundred times more painful and soreful. Today his fate lay in the hands of Subodh. God is this unjust, and fate this severe!

After he calmed down a little, he called all the other clerks of the office and told them about the order – "Henceforth all of you beware of yourselves. Subodh Chandra is not a person who can pardon offendors."

One of the clerks asked, "Is he very strict?"

Madaarilal replied with a smile, "you will know that in 3-4 days. Why should I complain about anybody? I just warned you to control yourselves. The man is very efficient but very short-tempered and arrogant. His nose is always up in anger. He may swallow thousands of rupees but will not even belch a little; but is too clever to let any subordinate swallow even a penny! Only God can save us from such a man! I am thinking of applying for leave and going home. I have to record my attendance at his home twice a day! From today, all of you are not Government servants but the Seretary's servants! While one of you may have to teach his sons, another might have to go the market to fetch grocery and cosmetics, while yet another might have to read the newspaper for him! And what to say of peons, who may never be seen in the office in future!"

This way, Madaarilal cooled himself by insinuating all the employees against Subodh Chandra.

After a week, when Subodh Chandra got out of his train, he was received by all his subordinates. They had all gone there to welcome him. The moment he saw Madaarilal, he hugged him and said, "Hey! You ….here…! Fantastic! How come you are here? It seems like ages since we met!"

Madaarilal said, "I am a head clerk in the Zilla Board. Hope you are fine!"

Subodh – "Oh my! Don't you mention! I went around so many places- Basra, France, Egypt and so many places. It is very heartening to know that you are in this office. I was totally lost as to how I am going to get things done here. I am totally blank; wherever I go, my good fortune follows me. In Basara, all the officers were very happy. In France too, I enjoyed a lot. In two years, I was able to make 25000 rupees and squandered every rupee. On returning from there, I was whiling away my time at the office of cooperative societies for a few days. I come here and meet you! (Looking at the other clerks) Who are these people?"

Madaarilal's heart was green with jealousy! 'Cunning chap! Has made 25000 rupees in France! My hand sores writing for hours together and I could not even make a few hundred rupees here!' He said, "Employees of our office. They have come to greet you."

He shook each employee's hand and said, "you have taken unnecessary pains to come over here. I am very grateful to you. I hope you gentlemen have no complaints against me. Treat me not as your officer but as your own brother. All of you work as a good team and ensure that the image of the Board remains bright and I can be comfortable. Your head clerk is my old childhood friend."

One smart clerk said, "we are all your obedient subordinates Sir. Knowingly we will never make you unhappy. But after all we are human; if at all we commit any mistake, you may please excuse us."

Subodh politely replied, "this is my philosophy and this has been my philosophy always. Wherever I went, I remained friendly even with my subordinates. All of us are the servants of a third party. So, what about arrogance or superiority? Yes. We have to discharge our duties honestly."

After all the employees wished Subodh and were returning, they started talking amongst themselves, "he seems to be a good man."

"The head clerk described him in such a way that he would eat us alive."

"In the beginning, everybody talks this way."

"This is just to project a good image."

One month passed by after Subodh took charge. Clerks, orderlies, peons and everybody was happy with his style of functioning. He was so cheerful and friendly that anybody who met him once turned out to be his friend forever. He never uttered a single arrogant word. He did not sound even refusals or rejections in an unfriendly manner. But in the eyes of hatred, good nature seems even more dangerous. All these ways of good behavior seemed irritating in the eyes of Madaarilal. He kept scheming some secret plan or the other against Subodh. First he tried to provoke the employees against Subodh but failed miserably. He tried to do that with the members of the Board but there too he had to accept defeat. He tried defaming Subodh among the contractors but he was ashamed by his failure there too. He wanted to ignite the dry grass and watch the fun from a distance! He mingled with Subodh very cheerfully and chatted with him like a true friend but kept himself busy scheming against him. Subodh had all good qualities but he could never recognize the true colours of men. He still took Madaarilal to be his good old friend.

One day, Madaarilal entered the Secretary's cabin and found the seat empty. Subodh had gone out on some duty. He found a bundle of five thousand rupees on the table. Some wooden furniture had been made for the Board's schools. The money was towards the cost of that furniture. The contractor was asked to come to take his payment and Subodh had withdrawn the cash for that purpose. Madaarilal peeped into the verandah and found no sign of Subodh. His honesty went for a toss! Greed joined along with jealousy. With shivering hands, he took the bundle of cash and filled both his trouser pockets with the same. Immediately he emerged out of the cabin and spoke to the peon in a loud voice, "Is Babu inside?" The peon was in a good mood that he could collect some tips from the contractor. Running back from the pawn shop outside, he said, "he was talking to someone in the office and just went out."

Madaarilal went into the office and told a clerk, "go show this file to the Secretary."

The clerk went with the file and returned in a few minutes, "Secretary Sir is not in the cabin. I have placed the file on his table."

Madaarilal said with a contracted face, "why does he have to leave his cabin unlocked like this and go out? Some day he may get cheated."

The clerk said, "who else other than office staff members go into his cabin?"

Madaarilal said in a sharp voie, "so, is every employee of this office a God? Nobody can say when a person can turn dishonest. I have seen even most honest people turning dishonest over petty sums. Right now all of us are very good. But nobody can easily escape temptation. That is human nature. Go and shut both the doors of his cabin."

The clerk took this lightly and said, "the peon is sitting at the door."

Madaarilal said angrily, "do as I say. Why do you say the peon is at the door? Is the peon some saint or sadhu? What he himself steals something? What can you do? His deposit is just three hundred rupees! Here each file is worth lakhs of rupees."

Saying this, Madaarilal got up, went and closed both the doors of the office. After he calmed down, he stealthily put the cash into one of the almirahs and continued his work seriously.

Subodh Chandra returned after about an hour. He saw the doors of his cabin shut. He went into the office and asked with a smile, "who shut my cabin doors? Friends, am I dismissed?"

Madaarilal stood up and politely naying that statement, said, "Saheb, excuse me! Whenever you go out of your cabin, even if it just for a minute, please do shut the doors and go. Important

Government papers, files and cash lie on your table. Who knows when a person might turn dishonest! I just heard that you had gone out and so I shut the doors."

Subodh Chandra opened his cabin, went in and started smoking a cigar in a relaxed mood, totally forgetting about the money that was on his table.

Just then the contractor arrived and greeted him. Subodh stood up, greeted him and sat back, "you are quite late. I was waiting for you. I had withdrawn cash at ten in the morning. Have you brought the receipt?"

Contractor – "Sir, I have brought the receipt."

Subodh – "then take your money and you may go. I am not happy with your work. You have not used good wood and there is no finesse in your workmanship too. If you continue to do such shoddy work in future, I will get you unlisted from the list of contractors."

Saying so, he looked at the table and did not find the bundle of cash there. He thought it might have got stuck between some files. He searched by moving all the papers and files but could not find the cash. "Where has the cash vanished? I had kept the bundle right here just a few minutes ago. Where can it go?" He looked between all the files. His heart started beating faster. He had searched thoroughly among all the papers on the table but the bundle was missing. He sat down on his chair and recollected all that had happened in the previous half hour. 'The peon came and handed over the bundle of cash to me. I remember that very clearly. How can such an important matter be forgotten and that too so soon! I accepted the bundle and kept it right here on the table, without even counting it. Then the advocate came in. He is my old acquaintance and hence we started chatting and walked upto that tree outside. He ordered for *pan* and we waited for that. It was a very brief interval. When I left the cabin, the bundle was very much here. I can remember well. Then where has the bundle vanished now? I did not lock it in a drawer or brief case or almirah. So, where can it go? Maybe somebody in the office has kept it aside safely. That can be the only possibility. I am panicking unnecessarily.'

He immediately went to the office and told Madaarilal, "have you by any chance removed the cash from here and put it in somewhere?"

Madaarilal said with a shock, "what, had you left some cash on your table? I don't even know that. Just now Pandit Sohanlal went in with a file but did not find you there. Only then I came to know that you went out talking with somebody and shut your cabin doors. What, are you not able to locate some cash?"

Subodh widened his eyes and said, "Arre sahib! Five thousand rupees! Just a few minutes ago, I had it withdrawn from the bank."

Madaarilal beat his forehead and said, "Five thousand rupees! Oh God! Did you search properly on your table?"

"Oh my! I have been searching for the last fifteen minutes."

"Did you enquire with the peon as to who all visited your cabin?"

"Please come. All of you help in this search. I am very upset."

All the employees entered the cabin and started looking out for the cash. All the almirahs, drawers and brief cases were looked into. Even the ledgers and registers were moved around and scanned through. There was no sign of the cash. There was no doubt that somebody had flicked the cash. Subodh took a deep breath and sat on his chair. His face turned pale and sick. Whosoever saw him in that state would think he had been sick for months.

Madaarilal said with sympathy, "very strange! No such thing had happened until today. I have been working in this office for the last ten years and never has even a penny been lost. I should have warned you on the very first day to be cautious about money matters but what to do? It never occurred to me then, as I never forsaw it. I am sure some outsider camc in and stole the cash. The peon should not have let anybody inside the cabin. It is his negligence. Even if he swears one lakh times that no outsider came in, I will not accept. From here, only Pandit Sohanlal went towards the cabin but he too peeped in and returned when he did not find you."

Sohanlal clarified, “I did not even step into your cabin Sir. I swear on my young son for this.”

Madaarilal said with wrinkled forehead, “why are you simply swearing? Did anybody say anything to you?” Then he whispered into Subodh’s ears, “if there is balance in the bank, first draw the money and pay this contractor. Or else it will become a shameful issue. We have lost the money already, why lose our honour too?”

Subodh said in a touching tone, “the bank balance may be just a few hundreds brother! Why would I worry so much if there was a balance there? I would have convinced myself that I squandered thirty thousand instead of twenty five thousand! The situation is such that there is not a penny even to buy a shroud for the corpse!”

Subodh Chandra committed suicide the same night. It was difficult for him to arrange for such a huge amount. He had no other way to hide his grief other than with the curtain of death.

Early next morning, the peon came to Madaraalal’s house and called him out. Madaarilal had not slept throughout the night. He came out with a shock. The peon said, “a very unfortunate thing has happened. The Secretary sahib has slit his throat with a knife in the night.”

Madaarilal’s eyes raised, face paled and his entire body was shivering such that he was struck by lightning.

“Slit with a knife?”

“Yes sir. We came to know only in the morning. The police have arrived. They want you there.”

“The dead body is still there?”

“Yes. The body will be sent for post-mortem shortly.”

“Are there too many people there?”

“All high officials have gathered there. There is no way one can peep at the corpse! He was such a gem of a person! Everybody is in tears. He has two little boys and a teenage daughter to be married. However much people try to control her, the wife keeps running to the body. There is none who is not wiping the tears with his handkerchief. He came very recently but became close to everybody. He never cared for money. He was very generous."

Madaarilal felt dizzy. Had he not supported himself against the doorway, he would have fallen down. He asked, "Was his wife weeping too much?"

"Don't even ask me *huzoo*r! It's like how the dry leaves continuously fall from a tree! Her eyes are red and swollen."

"How many sons did he have?"

"*Huzoor*, two sons and a daughter."

"The missing cash must also be a topic of discussion."

"Oh yes! Everybody feels it must be an insider's job. The constable wanted to arrest Sohanlal; maybe they may do so after discussing with you. The secretary *sahib* has stated in his dying statement that he does not suspect anybody."

"Has the secretary *sahib* left a written statement?"

"Yes. Maybe just before he slit his throat, he realized that all the employees may be in trouble in the morning and thus he wrote a letter to the collector."

"Has he said anything about me in the letter? Would you somehow know?"

"*Huzoor*, what do I know? But everybody has been saying that he has praised you a lot in the letter."

Madaarilal's heart started beating faster. He shed two big drops of tears. Wiping his tears, he said, "we both had studied together for nearly 8-10 years. We were always together whether for studying, playing, eating or chit-chatting. We were just like real brothers. What has he praised me for in the letter? How would you know?"

"Anyway, you are coming with me. Find out for yourself."

"Have all the arrangements for the last rites made?"

"No *sahib*. Didn't I tell you that the body will be sent for post-mortem? Okay. Please come soon, lest somebody else might be sent to fetch you."

"Everybody from our office must have reached there."

"Yes Sir. At least everybody from this locality was already there."

When Madaarilal reached Subodh Chandra's house, he felt as though everybody was looking at him suspiciously. The police inspector called him immediately and said, "you too record your witness note. We have taken the notes from everybody else."

Madaarilal wrote his note so cautiously that the police official was astonished. He had a slight suspicion on him but his note cleared it all fully.

Just then the two sons of Subodh came to Madaarilal and said, "please come. Amma wants to meet you." They were familiar with Madaarilal, as he used to visit them almost every day, though he had never entered the house anytime, because Subodh's wife veiled herself from outsiders. Now on being called by her his heart missed a beat, 'hope she is not doubting me! Hope Subodh has not expressed any such suspicious matter about me to her!' With a bit of hesitation and fear, he entered the home. When he heard the pathetic wailing of the widow, he was chocked with sorrow. As soon as she saw him, another dam seemed to have breached and tears started flowing from the eyes of the hapless woman. The daughter ran and held on to his feet. Both the boys too hugged him. Madaarilal could not bear to see the intense sorrow and solicitation of the oppressed in their eyes. His conscience started pricking him. He had cut the throat of the very people who trusted him so much, loved him so muh and treated him as their friend in need! He had been the cause for the crumbling of such a lovely family. What would become of these helpless people? The girl had to be married off. Who will carry out that duty? Who will bring up these boys? He was so numb with sorrow that not a word of consolation came out of his mouth. He felt his face had been blotted and his stature suddenly shortened! When he stole the cash, he never imagined that it would result in such a great tragedy. He just wanted to cause some impediment for Subodh but he never intended to ruin him completely.

The grief-stricken widow said in a quivering voice, "He has abandoned us in the middle of a river. Had I known he was planning to do such a thing, I would have surrendered everything that I have to him. He kept telling us that there will be some way out of this muddle. He wanted to approach some money-lender through you. I cannot tell you how much he trusted you."

Madaarilal felt like someone was piercing his heart with a lance. He felt something was getting stuck in his throat.

Rameshwari continued, "while going to bed he was in a very jolly mood. Like any other day, he drank milk, spent a good time with the children, played on the haromonium for some time, washed his mouth and then went to bed. There was nothing that gave the slightest indication of his intention. Seeing me worried, he said, 'You are worrying unnecessarily. I am an old friend of Madaarilal. After all when will he be of help to me but at such a time? He has played with me. He knows everybody around this town. Some arrangement will be made for the money.' But then I don't know when this thought of killing himself occurred to him! Unfortunately, I slept through the night like a log without even snoring. How do I know that he is going to play around with his life?"

Madaraalilal felt like the entire world was floating before him. He tried his level best but could not control his tears.

Rameshwari wiped her tears and said, "Bhaiyyaji, whatever had to happen has happened. But you must definitely find out who that cheat is, who ruined our lives. It is the handiwork of somebody from this very office. He was an angel. He used to tell me that he doubted nobody in the office, though it seemed like the handiwork of some insider only. My only request to you is to ensure that the sinner is not allowed to go scotch-free. The police may accept some bribe and spare him. They dare not do that before you. Whoelse do we have other than you, to now save our souls? To whom should we confide? It is fated that his dead body had to undergo this torture too!"

For a moment Madaarilal felt he should confess. 'I should clearly tell her I am that cheat, that abysmal fellow, that wicked creature! I shall fall at the feet of the widow and tell her to cut the throat of this sinner with the same knife.' But not a word came out of his mouth. Sitting thus with these thoughts, he felt giddy and fell down.

By evening, the post-mortem got over. The hearse proceeded towards the river. The entire office staff, all the higher officials and thousands of others followed the hearse. The pyre had to be lit by the sons but they were minors. So the widow was getting ready to perform the rite, when Madaarilal went to her and said, "let me carry out this rite. If you get busy with the rituals, who will take care of your children? Subodh was my brother. During his lifetime I could do nothing good to him; allow me to fulfil some duty as a friend of his at least on his death. After all I too owe something to him!" Rameshwari wept and said, "God has blessed you with a very generous nature Bhayyaji; otherwise, who cares to show concern to the family of dead? All the employees were standing there until midnight with folded hands and not one of them even offered to do this just to console me."

Madaarilal performed the last rites. He performed all the rites for all the thirteen days. On the thirteenth day the final rite of offering *pind* (a ball of rice with sesame seeds) to the departed soul was performed; a feast was offered to the Brahmins; beggars were served free meals and all the friends were hosted a lunch, all at the expense of Madaarilal. Rameshwari felt very much obliged and said, "whatever you have done for us this far is a lot enough. I do not want to burden you anymore. How much more do you need to do to fulfil your duty as a friend?" But Madaarilal did not listen to her. His fame spread far and wide – this is how a true friend should be!

On the sixteenth day, the widow told Madaarilal, "Bhayyaji, we will ever be indebted to you for all that you have done for us. Had you not shown concern on us, God knows what would have been our fate! There was not a soul to help us. Please let us go to our home-town now. The cost of living will be lower there and I would do a bit of farming too. These days of struggle will somehow pass away. Please continue to show your affection on us."

Madaarilal asked her, "how much of property do you have in the village?"

Rameshwari, "nothing great; we own a *kutcha* house and about 5 or 6 acres of leased land. He had just started construction of a *pucca* house but the money was not sufficient. It is left unfinished. We have already spent about 10 to 12 thousand rupees but the roof is yet to come up."

Madaarilal – "is there some money deposited in the bank? Or farming is the only source?"

Rameshwari- "there is not a paise of saving Bhayyaji. He was a spendthrift. Not a paise would remain in his hands. Just farming remains the only source."

Madaarilal – "do you think the yield on that land would be sufficient for your maintenance as well as the taxes?

Rameshwari- "what else can we do now Bhayyaji? We have to lead our life someway or the other. But for these children, I would have consumed some poison."

Madaarilal – "your daughter has also to be got married."

Rameshwari – "I am not worried about her marriage now. I may find some match among the farmers, who will wed her without seeking for dowry."

Madaarilal thought for a moment and said, "will you agree to a suggestion of mine?"

Rameshwari – "Bhayyaji, why would I not agree to your suggestion? Who else do I have?"

Madaarilal – "Then, instead of going to your village, come with me. Your children will grow like my children. You will face no problem. God willing, your daughter will also be wedded to a groom from a good lineage."

Rameshwari's eyes welled up. She said, "But Bhayyaji, think over ……" Madaarilal cut her short and said, "now I do not have a second thought. I will not accept any excuse. Don't families of two brothers live together? I considered Subodh as my brother and he will remain so forever."

None of her excuses were heard. Madaarilal took all of them to his house and for the last ten years he has been taking care of them. Both the boys are studying in college and the girl got married into a very reputed family. Madaarilal and his wife serve Rameshwari whole-heartedly and fulfil her interests. Madaarilal is offering his penance by this service, for the sin committed by him.

Separation

This is the story of a family belonging to the lower middle class splitting and getting back. It has interesting descriptions of small little issues and selfish motives that are normally seen in such families.

It spelt his doom for Bhola Mahato's son Raggh*u*, when Bhola Mahato married again on the death of his first wife. Ragghu was just ten years old then. He was happily playing *gulli-danda* (a regional game played with a small wood-stick and a longer one to beat it) in the village. The moment his step-mother entered, he had to start slogging. Panna was a beautiful woman. Beauty and pride always go hand in hand like a pair of skirt and blouse. She never soiled her hands with household chores. Ragghu had to remove the cattle dung, feed fodder to the bullocks and wash the vessels. Bhola totally changed and he found only negative points in Ragghu. He blindly listened to Panna's words, as was the custom those days. He did not pay any attention to Ragghu's complaints. The result was that Ragghu stopped complaining. Whom could he confide to? It was not just his father, but the entire village stood against him. 'He is a very adamant child. He never understands Panna. The poor lady pampers him by feeding him, which is why he has become such a boy. No other woman in her place would have managed the show. Only because Panna is such a simple and humble lady is she able to carry on.' People listen to only strong people; nobody cares for the laments of a weakling. Ragghu's heart was moving away from his mother day by day. Eight years passed by and Bhola Mahato too met his death.

Panna had four children – three sons and a daughter. So many mouths to feed but none to earn. Why would Ragghu care? It was as expected. He would marry and go away with his wife! The wife would only add fuel to the fire! Panna felt darkness engulfing her.

‘Whatever it is, I would not remain in the same house leaning on Ragghu’s support. I will not become a servant of the same house which I once ruled as a queen. I will not look at the face of the boy, whom I treated as my slave.’ She was beautiful and was not too old. She was in the pink of youth. Can she not find another home? But that would be difficult. People will laugh at her. Let them do so! It was nothing new in her community. She was not a Brahmin or Thakur to be shamed! It only happens in the upper castes that inside the house anything may happen but everything will be veiled farcically from the outside world! She could openly remarry and why would she remain as Ragghu’s dependent?

One month passed by after Bhola’s death. It was evening time. Panna was immersed in her thoughts when she suddenly realized her sons were not at home. It was the time when the cattle return home. She was worried the little boys may get trampled over by some bullocks. Who is at the door now to take care of them? Ragghu hardly acknowledges the presence of my boys. He never ever talks to them in a friendly manner. She came out and what did she see? Ragghu was sitting in the hut opposite to the house and making pieces of sugarcane. The boys stood looking at him and the girl was riding on his back, holding his neck with her tender hands. Panna could not believe her eyes. This was something new. Maybe he is showing off to the world that he loves his brothers too much, with evil thoughts in his mind! At an opportune moment, he might even kill them! He is a black viper! A black viper! She harshly said, “What are you all doing over there? It is sunset time, the cows will be returning.”

Ragghu spoke politely, “When I am right here *kaaki,* why should you worry?”

The older son Kedar said, “Kaaki, Ragghu *dada* has made two carts for us. Look at these. On one Khunnoo and I shall sit and on the other Lachman and Jhuniya will sit. *Dada* will drag both the carts.”

Saying so, he brought out two carts from a corner. Each cart had four wheels. The carts featured cushion for comfortable seating and side arms serving as brakes.

Panna was surprised and asked, “who made these carts?”

Kedar replied with irritation, "Who else? Ragghu *dada* has made them. He borrowed an adze and chisel from Bhagat's house and made these carts in no time. It runs so well *kaaki*! Sit down Khunnoo, I shall drag."

Khunnoo sat on the cart and Kedar started pulling it. The cart made a noise char-char and it seemed like it also joined in the game along with the boys.

Lachman sat on the other cart and said, "*Dada* pull."

Ragghu put Jhuniya also on that cart and ran pulling it along. All the three children started clapping their hands. Panna stood watching this scene with astonishment and wondered whether this was the same Ragghu that she had known!

After some time both the carts returned. The boys went into the house and started exchanging their experiences of their journey on the carts. They were so happy as though they had travelled by an aeroplane!

Khunnoo said, "*Kaaki*, all the trees were running."

Lachman-"And how the calf was running! All of them ran."

Kedar – "*Kaaki*, Ragghu *dada* pulls both the carts at the same time."

Jhuniya was the youngest. She expressed her happiness by jumping happily and dancing around, clapping her hands.

Khunnoo – "Now we shall get a cow for our house *Kaaki.* Ragghu *dada* has asked Girdhari to get us a cow. Girdhari said he will get the cow tomorrow."

Kedar – "The cow yields three *seers* of milk *kaaki*. We shall drink a lot of milk."

Just then Ragghu too entered the house. Panna looked at him with disdain and asked, "Ragghu, have you asked Girdhari to get us a cow?"

Ragghu replied apologetically, "Yes, I have requested him. He will get it tomorrow."

Panna – "From where will you get the money? Have you thought about that?"

Ragghu – "I have thought of everything *kaaki*. Don't I have this gold pendant? It will fetch twenty five rupees. I will deduct five rupees towards the cost of the calf and the cow will be ours."

Panna was stunned. Even her suspicious mind could not reject Ragghu's loving, good nature. She said, "why do you want to sell that pendant? What is the hurry to buy a cow now? When we have enough money on hand, we shall buy. Your barren neck will not look good. Did the boys not grow up without a cow at home all these days?"

Ragghu philosophically said, "*Kaaki*, this is the age for the boys to eat and drink well. If they cannot eat now, when can they eat? I don't feel great wearing that pendant. People might comment, 'father is dead; this fellow is roaming around with a pendant.'"

Bhola Mahato had died with the longing for a cow. He could never make that kind of money and the cow never came. He was helpless. How easily Ragghu had found a solution to that great worry! For the first time in her life, Panna was filled with trust on Ragghu. She said, "when you do want to sell jewelry, why sell your pendant? Take my chain."

Ragghu – "No way *kaaki!* That looks nice on our neck. What difference does it make for a man whether he wears a chain or not?"

Panna – "Come on! I have become an old woman. Why do I need a chain now? You are still young. Your neck will not look good without a chain."

Ragghu said with a smile, "are you already old? Who can match your beauty in this village?"

Ragghu's simple presumption made Panna shy. Her dry and haggard face was red with happiness.

Five years went by. There was no other farmer in the village who was as hard-working, honest and well-behaved as Ragghu. He never did anything against Panna's wish. He was now 23 years old. Panna kept pestering him, "Bhaiyya, go fetch your wife. How long will she stay with her parents? Everybody is talking ill of me, saying that I am not letting her come." But Ragghu kept delaying, "what's the hurry?" He had heard a lot about his wife's way of life and behavior through others. He did not want to get such a wife home and spoil his peace of mind.

Finally, Panna put her foot down one day, "so, you will not get her?"

"I have told you there is no great hurry."

"You may not be in a hurry but I am in a hurry. I am sending someone to fetch her, today."

"You will repent *Kaaki*; her ways do not suit us."

"For your own good, I will not talk to her at all. Then will she fight with thin air? After all she can take care of the kitchen. I am unable to manage the kitchen as well as the outside chores together. I will get her fetched today."

"If you wish to do so, carry on; then don't complain that instead of correcting her, I have become her slave."

"I won't say so. Go get a couple of sarees and some sweets."

Muliya arrived from her maternal home on the third day. She was received with melodious music on *shehnai* and *nagade* (kind of instruments played for happy occasions). The ritual of unveiling the face was performed. She seemed like a clear oasis in this desert. She was of wheat-complexion; she had large boat-like eyelids, pink cheeks and attractive eyes. Ragghu fell flat on seeing her!

Early in the morning, when she went out with a pot to fetch water, her wheatish complexion would turn gold and it seemed like the dawn was walking happily, with all its scents, pleasure and intoxication.

Muliya had come well prepared from her maternal home. 'My husband should toil night and day, while Panna relaxes like a queen and her sons roam around like the spoilt brats of the rich households.' She could not tolerate this. She would not be enslaved to anybody. Own sons are always own sons! How can they be true brothers to Ragghu? They will tag along Ragghu until they get wings. Once they become major, they will just fly away fluttering their wings, without even bothering about him.

One day she told Ragghu, "if you want to be a slave here, you may do so. I cannot do that."

Ragghu – "what shall I do then? You yourself think over. The boys are not yet old enough to take over the household responsibilities."

Muliya – "the boys are the queen's children, what are they to you? This is the woman who tortured you for every grain of food. I cannot stay put as a slave. I am totally in the dark about the income and expenditure. I wonder what you earn and what she does with all the money! You think the money is after all in the family; but beware, you may not get even a penny!"

Ragghu – "if I handover my earnings to you, imagine what the world will speak of me!"

Muliya – "let the world say what it wishes! I am not the property of the society! You will turn black with ill-fame smeared all over your face! You may die for the sake of your brothers! Why should I?"

Ragghu did not say anything. Whatever he feared of, had raised its head so soon! With a lot of coercion and efforts, he may be able to drag the matter for another six months or one year. After that his drama may not work. How long can the mother of a goat kid look after the welfare of its kid?(an idiom)"

One day Panna had spread some edible flowers for drying in the sun. The rainy season was on. The food in the grannery was getting damp. Panna said to Muliya – "*Bahu*, please be alert. I will go, bathe in the lake and come back soon."

Muliya replied casually, "I am feeling sleepy. You sit and watch. What if you do not bathe for one day?"

Panna placed back her saree and did not go to the lake. Muliya's provocation went waste!

After a few days, one evening Panna returned home after working in the farm. It was already dark. She had gone hungry throughout the day. She hoped her daughter-in-law would have made hot *rotis*. But when she came home, she was stunned to see that the hearth was cold and the children too were suffering hunger. Panna enquired in a low tone, "the stove is not lit until now?"

Kedarsaid, "today the stove was not lit even in the afternoon *Kaaki*. *Bhabhi* did not cook anything today."

Panna – "then didn't you all eat anything at all?"

Kedar – "there were a few left-over *rotis* from last night which Khunnoo and Lachman ate. I ate some parched grain."

Panna – "What about *bahu*?"

Kedar – "She has been sleeping. She has not eaten anything."

Panna lit the stove and started cooking. She was weeping as she mixed the dough for *rotis*. What a fate? She had slogged all day long in the field and in the night she has to slog it out in the kitchen.

Kedar was running fourteen years of age. Seeing his *bhabhi*'s idiosyncrasies, he could understand all about the family politics. He said, "*Kaaki*, *Bhabhi* no longer wants to live with you."

Panna got a start and asked, "does she say anything?"

Kedar – "She never says anything but that is what is bothering her. Why don't you let her go? Let them live as they like. We too have our God to take care of us."

Panna bit her tongue with her teeth and said, "stop it! Never ever utter such things in my presence. Ragghu is not your brother but your father. If I ever hear that you spoke to Muliya, I will consume poison."

The festival of Dussehra arrived. A fair used to be organized a little away from the village in a neighbouring village. All the village boys went to the fair. Panna too got ready to go with her sons and daughter. But she had no money. The savings were with Muliya.

Ragghu told Muliya, "the children are going to the fair. Give them all two paise each."

Muliya raised her eyebrows and said, "there is no money at home."

Ragghu – "Just recently I sold the grains. Has all the money been spent already?"

Muliya – “Yes. It is gone.”

Ragghu – “How can it go? Let me hear! You mean to say these boys cannot go to the fair on this festive day?”

Muliya – “Go tell your *Kaaki* to remove her money out; what will she do hoarding it?”

The keys were hung on a nail and just when Ragghu removed the keys and wanted to check the box, Muliya held his hand and said, “hand over the keys to me or else! We need to spend on their food, on their books and now for them to go to the fair. We are not earning for others to eat and smear the left-overs over our faces.”

Panna told Ragghu – “Bhaiyya, why worry about money? The boys shall not go to the fair.”

Ragghu said with irritation – “Why will they not go to the fair? The entire village is going there. Only our children will miss it?”

Saying so, he released his hand, took out the money and gave it to the boys. But when he returned the purse to Muliya, she threw the purse in the courtyard and turned her face and lay down. The children did not go to the fair!

Even after two days since this happened, Muliya did not eat anything and Panna too remained hungry. Ragghu tried his best to console Muliya and Panna but both of them never yielded. Finally he got worried and asked Muliya, “utter something! What is it that you want?”

Muliya said, facing the ground, “I do not wish anything. Just send me back to my house.”

Ragghu – “Okay. Get up and eat something. I will take you to your home.”

Muliya looked up at Ragghu. Ragghu was shocked to see her face! Where had that tenderness, that charm and grace gone? Her teeth were protruding out, eyes were jutting out and her nose ring was throbbing. Her eyes were red like fire. She said, “So, this is what *Kaaki* has taught you! This is the idea she has given you! After all I am not so new to this house! I can grind *moong* (green gram) on your roof! (This is an idiom meaning one can cause enough trouble) What do you think?"

Ragghu – "Okay! You may do so! But only if you eat something, will you get some strength to carry out your wish."

Muliya – "I will not even drink a sip of water until the house is split. I have borne enough. I can bear no more."

Ragghu was dumbfounded. He could not utter a word for almost a minute. He had never ever even in his wildest dreams thought that this house would split. He had seen a few families of the village breaking up. He had realized well that along with the hearth, the hearts too broke up. The near and dear become total strangers. They become like any other villager and no more relationship exists between them. He had decided then that he would never let such a disaster happen in his family but his determination was no match to the smartness of Muliya. 'Oh! She will spoil my image. The village will gossip that I could not keep the family united for even ten years after my father's death. From whom should I separate? Should I desert the children whom I carried, whom I brought up like my own and slogged night and day for their sake? Should I drive out my own kith and kin?' His throat was choked. In a quivering voice he said, "You wish that I separate from my own brothers? Think good! I will never be able to face anybody if I did such a thing."

Muliya – "But I cannot carry on with these people."

Ragghu – "Then you may go. Why are you trying to drag me out?"

Muliya – "Do you think I am feasting in your house? Is there no place for me in this vast world?"

Ragghu – "You may do as you please and live wherever you want. I cannot desert my family. The day two hearths start burning in this house, my heart will break into two and I cannot bear that pain. Whatever is bothering you, I can try to resolve that problem. You are the owner of all produce, all the money is with you. What else do you want? If you do not want to do any work, don't do. Had I been blessed enough, I would not have allowed you to even lift a pin. Your tender limbs are not made for physical work. But what can I do? Nothing is under my control. Even then, if you do not wish to work, do not work. But don't ever ask me to break this family. I plead with you."

Muliya bent her head out of her veil, came closer to him and said, "I am not scared of working. I do not wish to laze around and eat. I cannot bear anybody's authority. If your *Kaaki* is taking care of the home and doing all the household work, she does it for her own children. She is not favouring me. Then why should she show her authority? Her children may be her favourite but I have your support. I cannot tolerate to see that the entire family is comfortable and the children drink pots of milk while the person who is slogging it out to run the family gets to drink only dilute butter milk! Nobody is bothered about him. Just look at yourself! How weak you have become! The others will become sturdy young men in four years but if you continue like this, in another ten years, you will fall sick. Sit down! Why are you standing? Are you planning to kill me and flee? I will not forcefully take you away. Neither is this the order of a landlady! I tell you! You are really a stone-hearted man! Had I known that I would have to bear such a loveless treatment, I would never have come to this house. Even after I came, I should not have lost my heart to you. But now, I have become attached to you. Even if I go to my maternal home, my mind will be here. But You are least bothered about me."

These sweet words of Muliya did not affect Ragghu even a bit. He spoke in the same stern tone, "Muliya, I cannot do this. The very thought of breaking up the family causes a lot of pain to me. I cannot bear this injury."

Muliya mockingly said, "then why don't you wear bangles and sit inside? I shall wear the mustache! I thought you had some strength in you. But now I realise you are made of just mud!"

Panna stood in the passage, listening the two of them talking. She could not control herself anymore. She came to them and addressed Ragghu, "when she is so firm on separating, why are you trying to forcefully keep the family united? You go with her. God will take care of us. When Mahato died and we did not have even a leaf to protect us, it was God who managed the situation. Then why fear now? By God's grace, now all the three children are grown up. Nothing to worry."

Ragghu's eyes welled up and he said, *"Kaaki*, have you also lost your mind? Don't you know when the food gets divided, hearts too break up?"

Panna – "When she is not ready to change her stand, what can you do? If that is what God wills, nobody can do anything. We were together as long as we were fated to be together. Now, if she wishes only separation, let it prevail! Whatever you have done for my children, I shall never forget. Had you not taken charge of them, I don't know what would have been their fate today. I wonder at whose doorsteps, they would have been slogging or on which street they would be going around begging! I will sing your praise until my last breath. If my skin is required for making your footwear, I would willingly give it. We may live separately, but the moment the need arises and you call me, I will come running to you like a dog. You don't ever think that I would wish evil for you if you leave me. The day I hear of any misfortune afflicting you, I shall consume poison and kill myself. May God bless you with wealth, prosperity and progress! This thought shall emerge from every hair on my body until my death and if these children are truly their father's children, they too shall remain indebted to you forever."

After saying this, Panna left the place weeping bitterly. Ragghu stood staring at the sky and tears rolled down his cheeks.

After listening to Panna, Muliya felt that she had won and her status in the house was now established. She got up briskly, swept the floor, lit the stove and went to the well to fetch water. Her wish was fulfilled.

In the villages, women are of two groups – one in support of daughters-in-law and the other in support of mothers-in-law! The daughters-in-law went to their group for sympathy and suggestions, while the mothers-in-law approached their group! Both the groups meet separately. Muliya met a few daughters-in-law at the well. One of them asked, "today your old woman was crying a lot?"

Muliya replied with the pride of her victory, "she was the master of the house for this long. Who would not feel sad to give up their leadership position? Sister, I do not wish bad for her! But how long can a family run with the earnings of one man? After all, this is the age when I wish to eat well, dress well and enjoy life! Now you slog for her, then when our children arrive, slog for them! My entire life will be gone in misery and struggle!"

One daughter-in-law, "the old woman wishes that these two remain her slaves lifelong so that they can get fatter by the day!"

Another daughter-in-law: "on what trust can one die? When we cannot trust our own children these days, how can we trust others' children? When the children become independent, who will care for these two? They will only look at the faces of their own beloved! It is better to be cut and right at the beginning. There will be no complaint later on."

Muliya went back with the water, cooked and told Ragghu, "go bathe and come. The food is ready."

Ragghu never paid attention. He was holding his head in his hand and staring at the door.

Muliya – "what? Can you not hear me? I told you the food is ready. Go bathe."

Ragghu – "Yes. I can hear. Am I deaf? If the food is ready, you may eat. I am not hungry."

Muliya did not repeat. She went and put out the fire, piled up the *roties* in the netted bag and lay down with a long face.

In a while Panna came and said, "the food is ready. Bathe and eat. Muliya too must be hungry."

Ragghu angrily said, "*Kaaki,* will you let me stay at home or should I go away with a blemished face? Eating is always there! If I don't eat today, I can eat tomorrow. But I cannot eat now. Hasn't Kedar returned from the school?"

Panna – "He is yet to come. He may come in a while."

Panna understood that until and unless she cooked, fed her children and herself, he will not eat. Now she had to fight with Ragghu, abuse him and pretend that it was she who wanted to separate from them or else he will die worrying and repenting. She lit a second stove and started cooking. Meanwhile Kedar and Khunnoo returned from school. Panna said, "come on boys, the food is ready. Come and eat."

Kedar – "Shall I call *Bhaiyya* too?"

Panna – "You come and eat. *Bahu* has cooked separately for him."

Khunnoo- "Shall I at least go and ask him?"

Panna – "He will eat whenever he wants. You sit and eat. How are you concerned about such issues? Whoever feels like eating will eat and whoever doesn't feel so will not eat. When he and his wife are intent upon living separately, who can console them?"

Kedar – "So ammaji, should we live in a separate house? Why?"

Panna – "If they want let us live in one house; if not let them raise a wall across the courtyard."

Khunnoo went to the door and peeped out. He saw Ragghu drinking coconut water in the hay-hut on the opposite side.

Khunnoo – "*Bhaiyya* is drinking coconut water."

Panna – "He will eat whenever he feels like it."

Kedar – "Didn't *Bhaiyya* scold *Bhabhi*?"

Muliya was lying down in her room and listening to everybody. She came out and said, "*Bhaiyya* did not scold me. Now, you come and scold me."

Kedar turned pale. He did not reply. All the three boys ate their meals and went out. It was windy. The village boys and girls were picking the mangoes that had fallen off from the trees in the mango orchard. Kedar said, "let us also go and pick mangoes today. A lot of mangoes are falling off the trees."

Khunnoo – "*Dada* is sitting right here."

Lachman – "I won't come. *Dada* will be upset."

Kedar – "He has now separated from us."

Lachman – "Then if somebody attacks us, will he not come to protect us?"

Kedar – "Wah! Why would he not protect us?"

Ragghu saw all the three boys standing at the doorstep but did not say anything. Until then, he would scold them if they stepped out of the house, but today he sat unmoved. The boys now got some courage. They stepped out and went a few steps away from the house. Ragghu still did not speak up. How could he? He was moaning that *Kaaki* had already fed her children but did not bother to call him. Had she also lost her senses? What if I called the boys and they did not obey me? I cannot use force on them. They will roam around in this bad weather and what if they fall sick? Though his heart was full of concern for them, he did not utter anything. After the boys made sure that Ragghu will never stop them, they bravely went away.

Just then Muliya came and said, "Will you come in at least or still hold on to your point? For whose sake you were melting thus, she happily fed her sons, fed herself and is relaxing comfortably. 'My beloved did not enquire about me; I am called a newly-wed bride'! (lines from a Bhajan of Meera). Not once did she utter, 'come on *Bhaiyya*, come and eat.'"

Ragghu was experiencing extreme sorrow. Muliya's mocking harsh words added salt to his injury. With sorrowful eyes, he looked at her and said, "this is what you wished for. Go celebrate your victory."

Muliya – "No. I have served your meal and am waiting for you."

Ragghu – "Don't provoke me. Along with you I am also getting defamed. When you do not want to be friendly with anybody, why should somebody try pacifying you? Go ask *Kaak*i whether I should bring back the boys who have gone to pick mangoes."

Muliya showed her index finger at him and said, "now this man has to go! You have hundreds of reasons. You may go!"

Meanwhile, Panna came out of the house. Ragghu asked her, "the boys have gone to the orchard *Kaaki.* It is so windy."

Panna – "Now, who is there to control them? They may go to the orchard or climb trees or drown in the water! How much can I manage all alone?"

Ragghu – "Shall I go and fetch them?"

Panna – "When you are not going out of your own will, why should I ask you to go? If you wished, you could have stopped them. They went out right under your nose."

Even before Panna could finish her sentence, Ragghu kept aside the coconut and went towards the orchard.

When Ragghu returned with the boys, he saw Muliya standing near the hut. He said, "why don't you go and eat? I am not very hungry now."

Muliya mockingly said, "Yes. Why would you feel hungry? If your brothers have eaten, the food would have reached your stomach too!"

Ragghu grinding his teeth said, "don't you provoke me Muliya. The consequence will not be good. The food will not flee away. If I don't eat one time, I will not die. Do you think something very simple has happened at home today? It is not the hearth that you lit today but my heart! I was very proud that come what may, my house will remain one but today you damaged that pride of mine! Ill-fated day!"

Muliya said with irritation, "you have all the love and attachment! What about others? I have not seen anybody repenting like you."

Ragghu took a deep sigh and said, "Muliya, do not sprinkle salt on my wound. Only because of you, people gossip behind my back. If I am not attached to this family, who else will be? I have struggled to bring this family to this state. The boys who grew on my laps will become my competitors. I cannot even look at the boys, whom I used to reprimand with liberty, sternly. Even if I say something for their good, the society will comment that I am bossing over them. Please leave me alone. I cannot eat anything now."

Muliya – "I swear, you must silently come with me now."

Ragghu – "Even now it is not too late. Give up your adamance."

Muliya – "Drink my blood, if you do not want to eat your meal."

Ragghu closed his ears with his palms and said, "What a thing you uttered Muliya! I was just about to get up. Okay. I will come to eat. I have no patience to bathe now. But I want to clarify one thing to you. Even if I ate six *roties* in place of four and you even drown me in ghee, this fire which is burning in my heart will never get doused."

Muliya – "Oh! The fire will get doused. Everybody feels this way in the beginning. Don't you see how the soothing music of comfort is being played inside? She was after all wishing that somehow this separation happen! She is not the moon that she was, to swallow all that comes into the house!(an idiom meaning, she is not as innocent as she was earlier). Why would she want to live with us anyway?"

Ragghu said in a worried tone, "this is what is most hurting to me. I never expected *Kaaki* to behave this way."

Ragghu sat to eat but every morsel seemed like poison to him. It seemed like the *roties* were made of hay and the dal tasted like water. The water would never cross his throat and he did not even look in the direction of milk. He just ate a few pieces of *roti* and got up. He felt as though he was eating at the death ceremony of someone dear to him.

He did the same thing in the night too. He just kept up his word and actually did not eat his meal. He was restless throughout the night. He hallucinated that Mahato was sitting at the door. He woke up with a start many times during his sleep. He felt Bhola Mahato was looking at him with a scorn.

He was eating twice a day but as though he ate at an enemy's place. He could not forget the sorrowful image of Bhola. He could not sleep properly in the night. If at all he went into the village, he walked bending down his head and hiding his face, as if he had slaughtered a cow!

Five years passed by. Ragghu was the father of two sons. A wall was raised in the courtyard, the land was divided with bunds and the bullocks and calves were shared. Kedar was now nineteen years old. He had stopped schooling and started working on his land. Khunnoo took care of the cows. Only Lachman went to school. Panna and Muliya hated the sight of each other. Muliya's sons spent most of their time with Panna. She massaged them, dressed them up and carried around all the time but Muliya never uttered one nice word. Only Panna was interested in this. She did everything with a detached feeling. Her boys had started earning and her daughter was old enough to take care of the kitchen. She just helped her. In contrast to this was Ragghu's house, where he was the lone man to slog. He had become weak and battered and seemed much older than he actually was. He was just around thirty and his hair had turned grey. His back was bent. Incessant cough was consuming him. He was in a pitiable state. Farming involves a lot of hard work. He was not able to do full justice to farming. Therefore the yield was also meagre. He was in debt, which was bothering him a lot. He badly needed rest. He would have earned it after so many years of persistent hard work and he could have reduced his burden. But Muliya's selfishness and shortsightedness had destroyed the lush green fields. Had they all been together, he would have earned a pension and relaxed outside the house, sipping coconut water. His brothers would have taken care of the physical work, while he would have just given his advices. He would have spent time settling disputes or serving sadhus and saints. He had lost that chance forever. Now the burden of his worry was getting heavier by the day.

He started getting fever intermitantly. Heart burn, worry, hard work and poverty will after all result in sickness. In the beginning, he neglected it. He thought he would get well automatically but his condition worsened day after day and he had to treat himself. He would eat whatever anybody suggested. He had no means to go to a professional doctor. Even if he had money, what is the use of spending on medicines, when his illness needed rest and nutricious food too. Neither could he eat nutricious food nor sit back, relax and breathe fresh air. He got weaker.

Had Panna given a chance, she would have advised Ragghu. But now her sons did not even speak to him. Instead of helping him with medicines, they only made fun of him. 'Bhaiyya thought by living separately, he would hoard gold and silver. *Bhabhi* thought she would deck herself up in gold. Look at their state now! Who cares for them? They are sure to suffer and die! Too much of struggle too is not good. One should work only according to his capacity. One should not give up his life for money.'

Panna – "What is Ragghu's fault?"

Kedar- "Arre! I perferctly understand! Had I been in *Bhaiyya*'s place, I would have used a stick! It is a joke that he yielded to a woman's adamant behavior! It must have all been his own ulterior plan! Everything is so clear!"

One day Ragghu's flickering wick of life came to an end! Death brought peace to all his worried mind!

In his last moments, he sent words for Kedar but he had gone out to water the sugarcane fields. He feared that he might have sent for him to borrow some money for medicines. So, he found the pretext of watering the field, to avoid him.

Darkness engulfed Muliya's life. The base on which she had built the walls of her wishes had crumbled! The stake on account of which she was bragging around, was lost. The villagers commented, 'God has meted out instant punishment!' The poor woman was ashamed and wept bitterly, holding on to her two children. She had no courage to face anybody in the village. She felt every person was saying, "your feet were fleeting in the air out of pride! Finally, justice has been done!" How could she run the family now? Who will be her savior? Who would take care of the farming? Though her poor Ragghu was sick and weak, he did not shirk his duty until his death. Out of extreme fatigue, he would sit for a while, holding his head with his hands and then continue working. The farms were in a very bad state. Who will manage them now? Bags of foodgrains lay ready for being de-husked, in the grannery. Sugarcane fields had to be watered. How could she manage everything all alone? And ploughing is not a one-man job! From where will she get three labourers? There were hardly any person willing to labour on others' fields. There was a very fierce competition to get labourers. What could she do?

Thirteen days passed by. The final rites were done with. On the next day, Muliya carried her two children and went to the grannery to clean the foodgrains stored. She lay down one of her children on the grass under a tree and with the other sitting beside her, she started de-husking the grains. She was calling out the bullocks and crying. 'Has God created her only for this? How the tables have turned?' The grains were cleaned up at the same time the previous year too. She had taken juice and baked beans for him. Today, there was neither anybody over her nor below her! But she was not anybody's slave. She still did not repent having separated!

All of a sudden she heard her young one crying. When she peeped out she saw her other child trying to pacify him, "*Bhaiyya*, don't cry! Calm down!" He was trying to close his mouth gently and calm him. When the baby did not stop crying, he lay down beside him, put him on his shoulders and started patting him with love. When even that did not calm the child, he himself started crying.

Panna just then ran to the children, carried the younger one, kissed him and said, "Why didn't you leave the kids with me *bahu*? Oh my God! The poor thing is struggling on the ground. After I die you may do as you please. But I am still alive! By families breaking up, kids do not become strangers!

Muliya said, "you too did not have free time. What can I do?"

Panna – "What was the great hurry for you to come over here? The grains will not get destroyed. There are three boys in the family. When will they come of use? Kedar wanted to de-husk the grains yesterday but it was I who asked him to first go and water the sugarcane fields lest the crops may dry up. De-husking could wait for even another ten days. Since yesterday, he is irrigating the sugarcane fields. By the day after tomorrow that job will be done. Then this de-husking could be attended to. You would not believe how much Kedar is affected by Ragghu's death. He asks me almost hundred times a day, 'hope *Bhabhi* is not crying too much? Ensure the boys are not going hungry.' If any of your children cries, he comes running to me and says, 'go check why he is crying amma.' Yesterday he told me with tears, 'Amma, had I known *Bhaiyya* was going to depart so soon, I would have served him a bit.' The one who would wake up only on being woken up, is now waking up the early hours and going to work. Yesterday, when Khunnoo said, 'let us first irrigate our sugarcane fields and then attend to *Bhaiyya*'s, he scolded him so much that Khunnoo just shut his mouth. Kedar said, 'what is your sugarcane and our sugarcane? Had *Bhaiyya* not taken charge of us those days, we would have either been dead by now or be begging on the streets. Today you have become a big sugarcane trader! It is only because of his hard work that you have become a great man today!' Two days ago, when I went to call him for lunch,

Kedar was sitting in the hut and crying. I asked him 'why are you crying?' He replied, 'Amma, *Bhaiyya* died onlybecause of the pain of separation. He was not old enough to die. I don't know why these things didn't occur to me then! I would not have been angry with him."

Saying this, Panna looked at Muliya suggestively and said, "Kedar will not let you live separately *Bahu.* He says, 'if *Bhaiyya* laid down his life for our sake, we too will lay down our lives for the sake of his children.' "

Tears rolled down the cheeks of Muliya. She saw genuine grief, genuine solace and genuine concern in Panna's words. Never had Muliya's heart leaned towards Panna so much till this day. She, from whom she feared only mockery and revenge, turned out to be her generous well-wisher.

For the first time, Muliya felt ashamed of her selfhishness. For the first time her soul denounced separation.

Five years went by after this. Panna is now an old woman. Kedar is the master of the house and Muliya, the mistress. Khunnoo and Lachman are married but Kedar is still a bachelor. He says, "I will not marry." Many proposals came by and discussions took place but he never agreed. Panna allured him in many ways and spread a net but he never got entangled! He says, "what comfort does one get from women? Once the wives come into the family, the men's behavior changes totally! After that it's all about the wife! Parents, brothers, sisters-everybody becomes a stranger! When a person like *Bhaiyya* changed so much, then what to say of anybody else? God has blessed with these two boys. What else do I want? Without getting married, I have been blessed with two sons! What else do I need? Whosoever we consider as our own, becomes our own, while whosoever we treat as strangers remain strangers!"

One day Panna asked, "how will your lineage continue?"

Kedar – "My lineage is already continuing. I consider these two boys as my own."

PLanna – "If it is just by considering so, then you may be considering Muliya as your own wife!"

Kedar replied shyly – "You are ragging me amma."

Panna – "Why should I rag you? After all she is your *Bhabhi.*"

Kedar – "Why would she accept a rustic villager like me as her husband?"

Panna – "You first give me your assent and I shall ask her."

Kedar – "No my amma! What if she starts crying?"

Panna – "If you are willing, I will somehow try to guage her mind, casually".

Kedar – "I don't know. Do as you please."

Panna understood Kedar's motive. Her son has fallen for Muliya but is not able to express his feeling to her out of hesitation and fear.

The same day, Panna told Muliya, "what shall I do *Bahu*? Some our wishes remain only within our hearts! If Kedar too settles down with a wife, I would die without any worry."

Muliya – "He is not at all willing to marry."

PLanna – "He says he will marry only if he finds a woman who could live in harmony with everybody in the family."

Muliya – "Where can you find such a woman? Look out everywhere."

Panna – "I have already found one."

Muliya – "Really? Which village does she come from?"

Panna – "I will not reveal now! But I am sure that if she marries Kedar, this family will be a happy family and Kedar's life will become fruitful. I don't know whether the girl will give her consent."

Muliya – "Why wouldn't she consent Amma? Where can she get such a handsome, well-behaved and well-placed groom? He must have been a great sadhu or mahatma in his previous birth; or else who would remain a bachelor fearing domestic fights? Where does this girl live? Tell me and I shall go and convince her."

Panna – "If you wish, you can convince her. Only you can do it."

Muliya – "I will go right now, fall at her feet and get her consent."

Panna – "Shall I reveal? It is you."

Muliya shyly said, "Come on Ammaji! You are teasing me."

Panna – "Why tease you? After all he is your brother-in-law."

Muliya – "Why would he take an old woman like me as his wife?"

Panna – "He is waiting only for your consent! He is not interested in anybody else. He is not expressing his feeling to you out of fear. But I can read his mind."

Muliya's body, which was battered due to the pain of widowhood suddenly brightened up like a lotus. She felt like she won back all that she had lost in the last ten years, with interest! The same tenderness, the same brightness, the same attraction and the same sight!

The Pall (*Coffin*)

An interesting story which bares poverty layer by layer. Gheesu and Madhav consume liquor and non-vegetarian food out of the money meant for a pall. It describes very well, the impudence of human beings.

The father and son were sitting silently in front of a pile of ashes that lay after the fire they had lit to warm themselves up had consumed all the firewood, outside the hut. Bhudhiya, the young wife of the sonwas struggling in intense labour pain inside the hut. In between her scream was getting so unbearably painful that the two of them held their chest tightly. It was a cold winter night. The entire village was dark and silent.

Gheesu said, "I think she will not survive. The entire day she has been suffering. Just go have a look at her."

Madhav replied with irritation, "if she had to die, why cannot she die soon? What can I do by seeing her?"

"You are heartless. You are so insincere with the woman with whom you enjoyed life throughout the year!"

"I cannot bear to see her suffering and struggling out of pain like this."

It was a family of cobblers and had earned ill-fame all around. Gheesu lazed around for three Gheesu days, if he worked for one day! Madhav was such a lazy fellow that after working for just half an hour, hc whiled away his time for almost an hour, smoking. Therefore, nobody employed them. Even if they had just a handful of grain at home, they never went to work. When they had to go without food for 2 or 3 times, then would get on to a tree and chop a little wood and Madhav would go sell that wood. As long as they had that money on themselves, they roamed around the village. Not that there was no opportunity in the village. It was a village of farmers and hard-working men had fifty different jobs! But these two were offered work only when they had no other go but to accept the turnover of one man from two of them! Had they been sadhus, they did not require any special efforts of control and discipline for their happiness and guts! They had those traits –happiness and guts, naturally!

Their life was very strange! They had no asset other than a few clay vessels at home. They covered their bodies with tattered clothes. They were least bothered about the world and were deep in debts! They had no problem facing the rebukes or sometime even physical beatings! They were so useless that even though nobody had any hope of getting back their money, they lent them. They would steal peas and potato from others' fields, bake them and eat or steal a few sugarcanes from somebody's field and chew them in the night. Gheesu had spent his life of 60 years only in this great manner and Madhav followed his father's footsteps very loyally. In fact, he even overtook his father! Right now, they were busy roasting potato, that they had stolen from some field, in the fire in front of them. Gheesu's wife had died long ago. Madhav had got married the previous year. Since the lady entered this household, she had brought some order into it and somehow feeding the two useless guys. Thus after she entered the house, the two men became lazier. Not just that, they had even become more arrogant. If at all somebody calls them to work, they demanded double the normal amount as wages. That woman was dying of labour pain today and the two of them are eagerly waiting for her to die, so that they could sleep peacefully!

Gheesu removed the potato from the ashes and started peeling it. He said, "go and check out in what condition she is. This may be the curse of a witch! Even an occultist demands one rupee in this village."

Madhav feared that if he went into the hut, Gheesu might eat away a larger portion of the potatoes. He said, "I am scared to go inside."

"Why are you afraid? After all, I am right here."

"So, why don't you go in and check out?"

"When my wife died, I sat near her body for three days. Moreover, won't it be embarrassing to her if I went in? I have not even looked at her face till today. How can I go and see her in this condition? She will not even be conscious of herself! If she sees me, she cannot even freely move her limbs in pain."

"I am wondering what if a child is born? There is no oil, jaggery or flour at home. Absolutely nothing at home!"

"Everything will appear, if God wills! Those who refuse to give us even a rupee today, will themselves call us and offer money tomorrow. I had nine sons. Everytime the state would be the same – there would be nothing at home. But somehow God helped us cross the rough waters."

It was not very strange that these two were like this in a society, where the living conditions of farmers who worked hard were no better than their own and the people who were exploiting these farmers were getting richer by the day! In fact, Gheesu was more rational and sensible than all the ignorant farmers and hence instead of mingling with those farmers, he made his presence felt in intellectual meets! Of course, he did not have the ability to follow the principles or procedures of such meets. But he attended them just because he had realized that many of the participants in such meets held positions like the village chief, et al, though the entire village pointed fingers at them. Above all he had the satisfaction that even if they were not very well off, they need not slog like the farmers; and their simplicity and dissociation were not exploited by anybody! Both of them peeled hot potatoes and were hogging. They had not eaten anything since the previous day and hence had no patience to wait for them to cool. They were burning their tongues sometimes. When the potato gets burnt, its outer part burns the sensitive palate and throat and instead of holding it there, it is only better that one swallows it! In there, there are many enzymes that can cool it. That is why, both of them were swallowing the potatoes speedily, which brought tears in their eyes!

Gheesu at that time was reminded of Thakur's marriage, which he had attended twenty years before. The satisfaction that he got on that day was memorable enough and the memory was fresh till today. He said, "I cannot forget that feast! After that I have never got to eat such a tasty sumptuous meal in my life. The bride's family had fed everybody *puries* to their hearts' fill! The rich and poor all ate *puries* fried in pure ghee! Then there were *chutney, raitha,* three types of salads, one gravy of vegetables, curds, sweets and Oh, how can I explain to you the good taste of all those things; there was no obstruction of any sort; one could eat as much of whatever he wanted as he felt like! People hogged so much that they could not even drink a sip of water after that! But the people who served, again brought hot and tasty *kachories* and served everybody even if they refused! After washing our mouth, we also were given *paan* and cardamom. But I had no patience to eat it! I could not even stand up properly! I went home immediately and lay down on my blanket. That Thakur was so generous!"

Madhav relished all the dishes in his mind and said, "now, nobody feeds us such a meal."

"Why will anybody feed such a meal now? That was a different age! Now, everybody thinks of austerity. Don't spend lavishly in wedding celebrations or death ceremonies! Wonder where they hoard all that wealth that they earn by exploiting the poor! There is no limit of exploitation. But when it comes to expenditure, they become thrifty!"

"Would you have eaten at least twenty *puries*?"

"I ate more than twenty."

"I would have eaten fifty."

"I think I too would not have eaten less than fifty! It was so well fried. You could not have eaten even half of what I ate that day."

Both of them ate the potatoes, drank some water, lay down right there, covering themselves with their *dhoties* and crouching their bodies. They were lying like two well-fed pythons lying in coils, as if dead!

And Bhudhiya was still screaming with pain.

In the morning, when Madhav went into the hut, he found his wife cold. Flies were roving over her face. Her still eyes were suspended in one position. The entire body was smeared in dust. Her child was dead in her womb.

Madhav ran out to Gheesu. Then both of them started beating their chests and wailing aloud. When the neighbours heard them cry, as was the custom, they came there and tried to console the two of them.

But there was no time to cry too long. They had to think of the pall and firewood for the dead body. The money in their household was invisible like meat in a kite's nest!

The crying father-son duo ran to the Zamindar.He hated the very face of these two men. He had beaten the two of them on many occasions for various reasons like theft or not working as per their promise. He asked, "what happened Gheesu? Why are you crying? You are not even seen anywhere these days. I understand you do not wish to live in this village anymore."

Gheesu fell on the ground and said with tear-filled eyes, "I am in great difficulty. Madhav's wife died last night. She was suffering all through the night *sarkaar*. We both were sitting by her side. We kept giving her medicines and doing whatever best we could do but she disappointed us. Now, we have nobody who would give us even a single *roti*. We are devastated. Our household has totally crumbled. I am your slave! Who else but you can help me carry out her last rites? Whatever little we had, we spent on her treatment. Only with your generosity can her soul rest in peace! Where else can I go?"

Zamindar was generous. It was like trying to die a black blanket to sympathyse with Gheesu! He felt like driving him out. He would never turn up when I called for him and now when the need arose, he has come flattering him. Wretched, lazy fellow! But this was not the time to show his anger or punish him. He threw two rupees at him, grudgingly. He could not utter even a single consoling word. He did not even look at him. He dismissed him as though a big burden was relieved off his back.

When the Zamindar had given two rupees, how could the traders and money-lenders get the courage to refuse? Gheesu was very well-versed in singing praises of the Zamindar. Some of them gave two annas, while some four annas. In an hour, Gheesu had collected a handsome amount of five rupees. They got grains from here and firewood from there. In the afternoon, Gheesu and Madhav set out to the market to get the pall. The neighbours were preparing stretcher to carry the body, with bamboo and wood.

The kind-hearted women of the village came, looked at the dead body and shed tears at her terrible condition.

On reaching the market, Gheesu said, "Madhav, we have collected enough firewood to burn her body."

Madhav said, "Yes, there is enough firewood. We now need a pall."

"Okay! Let us buy some light pall."

"What else? It will be too late by the time the body is cremated! Who can see a pall in the darkness of the night?"

"What a bad custom! The one who does not even get a tattered piece of cloth to cover her body during her lifetime, required a new pall on her death!"

"The pall after all burns down with the corpse!"

"Then, what! Will it be saved? Had we got these five rupees a few days ago, we could have at least given her medical assistance."

Both of them were exchanging their views and going around in the market. They visited many cloth stores. They examined varieties of cloth – silk and cotton but were never satisfied. They did this till late evening. Then by some divine inspiration, they reached a toddy shop and entered it as though it was predetermined! For some time they stood perplexed. Then Gheesu approached the bartender and said, "Sahuji, give us also a bottle."

After that, they ordered for some munches and fish fries and sat in the verandah of the shop and peacefully drank the toddy.

After drinking a lot of toddy, they both were fully intoxicated.

Gheesu said, "what does one get by covering a body with pall? After all it just wastefully burns. Nothing goes with *bahu.*"

Madhav looked at the sky as if seeking the witness of the Gods above for his innocence, "it is the custom of the society that people dole out thousands of rupees to the Brahmins. Who checks whether one gets all that in the other world or not?"

"The rich and mighty have enough wealth. Let them blow up! What do we have to blow up?"

"But how will you answer people? Will they not ask you for the pall?"

Gheesu laughed, "Arre! Let us say the money slipped out of our waist and got lost. We searched for it but could not find it. People may not trust that but still they will give us more money."

Madhav also laughed at this unexpected opportunity and said, "she was such a good soul that on her death she got us to eat and drink to our satisfaction."

They had emptied almost half a bottle. Gheesu ordered for two seers of *puries*. He ordered for *chutney*, pickles and some non-vegetarian food too. The eatery was right in front of the toddy shop. Madhav quickly brought all the stuff in two leaves. They spent one and a half rupees in full. Now very little money was left with them.

The two of them were eating the *puries* so peacefully like a tiger eating its prey in a forest. They were least bothered about answering anybody or earning any ill-fame. They had won over all such feelings long ago.

Gheesu said in a philosophical tone, "Will she not earn *punya* if our souls are satisfied?"

Madhav lowered his head with devotion and seconded, "Of course she will! Oh God! You are omnipresent! Please take her to heaven! We both are heartily blessing her! We never ate such good food in our entire lives."

After a second Madhav raised a doubt, "*Dad*a, won't we also be going over there one day?"

Gheesu did not reply this innocent question. He did not want spoil the fun right now thinking of the other world!

"If we are questioned there as to why we did not give her a pall?"

"We shall just snub her."

"She will definitely ask."

"How do you say that she will not get a pall? Do you think I am such a fool? Am I just fooling around all these sixty years? She will get a pall, a very good one!"

Madhav could not believe. He asked, "Who will give? You have spent all the money. After all she will question me and not you. It was I who married her."

"Who will give, why don't you tell me?"

"The same people who have given all along! Yes, One thing;this time the money will not come to our hands."

As darkness set in and the stars started twinkling in the sky, the toddy shop was turning colourful. Some were singing, while some of them bragging around while a few others were hugging their friends. A few of them were throwing the empty pots on their friends' faces.

There was happiness in the atmosphere and the air was intoxicated. Many of them would get intoxicated just with one peg of toddy. More than the alcohol, the very atmosphere intoxicated them. The struggles of life brought them there and for some time they would be unaware of their existence. They would neither be dead nor alive!

The father-son duo were happily gulping peg after peg. Everybody was looking at them. How lucky were the two of them to have a big bottle in front of them!

After their hunger was fully satisfied, Madhav got up and handed over the left over *puries* to a beggar, who stood looking at them with hungry eyes. For the first time, they felt the joy, honour and satisfaction that one gets in the act of 'giving.'

Gheesu said, "Go and eat well. Bless on account of whom you got this today. She is dead. Your blessing will definitely reach her. Bless with all your heart, as this was earned the hard way."

Madhav once again looked at the sky and said, "she shall reach heaven and become its queen."

Gheesu stood up and felt as if he was sailing in the air. He said, "Yes my son! She shall go to heaven. She did not bother anybody or oppress anybody. She has fulfilled our lifetime wish on her death. If she does not go to heaven, do you think these fat men, who loot the poor with both their hands and bathe in the holy Ganga and offer the holy water in temples to wash away their sins, will go there?"

This colour of devotion suddenly changed. The very nature of intoxication is instability. It is a journey of sorrow and despair.

Madhav said, "But *dada*, the poor lady suffered a lot in her lifetime. She bore so much pain before her death." He closed his eyes with his palms and started crying with loud sobs.

Gheesu consoled him, "Why are you crying my son? She is relieved from this artificial world and is free from all struggle. She is fortunate that she could break away from this mortal world of materialism."

Both of them stood and sang, "Hey, wife of the dupe! Why are you twinkling?"

All the drunkards were gazing at them, as the two of them were singing with intoxication. They started dancing too. They jumped and skipped, fell down and rolled over. They expressed with animation. Finally they fell flat fully intoxicated!

❏❏❏